A NEW EMPIRE

A FOG CITY NOVEL

LAYLA REYNE

A New Empire

Copyright © 2019 by Layla Reyne

Cover Designer: Cate Ashwood, Cate Ashwood Designs

Cover Photography: Wander Aguiar, Wander Aguiar Photography

Layout: Leslie Copeland, LesCourt Author Services

Professional Beta Reading: Leslie Copeland, LesCourt Author Services

Developmental Editing: Kristi Yanta, Edits by Kristi

Copy Editing: Keren Reed, Keren Reed Editing

Proofreading: Susan Selva, LesCourt Author Services

First Edition

November, 2019

E-Book ISBN: 978-1-7341753-0-1

Paperback ISBN: 978-1-7341753-1-8

Content Warnings: explicit sex; explicit language; violence.

ABOUT THIS BOOK

Legacies were made to be rewritten.

Assassin Hawes Madigan wants to do right—by his family, his organization, his city, and the man he's falling for, ATF agent Christopher Perri. But Hawes's rules are being challenged by someone willing to kill for the old ways. To save his soul and his empire, Hawes must make an impossible decision: fight from the outside or bend the knee to win back his throne from within.

Chris is used to being the inside man, the one undercover. Now, he's on the outside marshaling forces in support of the man and the ring of assassins he was supposed to take down. His mission shifted when he found something that's been missing for ten long years—a home, with Hawes.

As Hawes and Chris make a dangerous play for control, the lines between allies and traitors blur. Trusting the wrong person could destroy the legacy Hawes envisions for the Madigans. But not trusting anyone, or each other, could mean lights out on their love and lives forever.

The King and King Slayer fight together in this thrilling conclusion to the *Fog City Trilogy*!

For LJ (and Ethan),
who showed me the way to lovable assassins.

CHAPTER ONE

The salvage boat, jacked as it was for smuggling, was more than fast enough to outrun the converging officers and agents. Hawes swung the boat around, gunned the engine, and disappeared into the night, the lights and shouts fading into the darkness behind him.

If only his conscience—his heart—was that easy to outrun.

Dante...*Chris*...was back there, shot and sinking in the cold, dark water. The only things that kept Hawes driving forward, kept him from yanking the wheel and turning the boat around, were the tracker he'd slipped into Chris's pocket, the flare he'd thrown into the Bay where Chris had gone under, and Kane's shouts as the chief had splashed into the water.

They would find him. It was a clean wound. He'd be fine.

And Hawes had another bleeding agent on deck to worry about. Not to mention the other bodies...

He withdrew two phones from his pocket. On the first, he texted Holt, alerting him to the tracker on Chris. Then he tossed that phone onto the deck, brought his heel down on it, and kicked the shattered pieces overboard. On the second, a burner, he texted an SOS to the single programmed contact. He had alerted her in advance and asked if she'd be willing to assist, in case he had to put certain contingency plans into motion. She was ready and waiting. Coordinates came back in less than a minute.

Ten minutes after that, Hawes maneuvered alongside a sleek yacht with Irish and American flags flying off the stern. He lowered the salvage vessel's anchor, killed the engine, and moved to greet the statuesque woman standing at the portside rail of the other boat.

"Went sideways?" Melissa Cruz asked, her dark eyes assessing the wreck of a deck Hawes had picked his way across. Bodies, blood, weapons.

"Sideways, upside down, briefly right side up, then underwater." Hawes tossed a mooring line to the former FBI Special Agent in Charge. In the private sector now, Mel handled security for Talley Enterprises and hunted down bounties on the side.

She secured the rope to the yacht's rail, helping to steady the two vessels so Hawes could extend a gangway between them. She was dressed down in jeans and a sweater, her dark curls piled in a bun atop her head, but casual wear did nothing to make her any less intimidating. Hawes knew of only one person who had ever bested Helena in hand-to-hand combat, and that person was standing across from him. "Sounds like an eventful night," she said.

"As expected." And unexpected in other ways—Reeves's involvement, Zoe's betrayal, Chris's change of heart, the unconscious agent Hawes now hefted into his arms. "We need to get him medical attention," he said, carrying ATF agent Scott Wheeler across the gangway to the yacht.

"I'm not set up here," Mel said, "but the *Ellen* has a full-scale infirmary. I can have a doctor meet us there."

"She's in dock?" Hawes was familiar with TE's shipping vessels, Madigan Cold Storage having custom-built or retrofitted the refrigeration units on most of them.

"Port of Oakland." She helped him get Wheeler situated. "They finished off-loading yesterday. Good timing."

That was about the only thing good right now. Hawes straightened, and his gaze strayed back to the salvage vessel. To Zoe lying dead next to Reeves and Gilbert. His breath caught, and heat stung the corners of his eyes, betrayal burning through him like a branding iron. So much betrayal littering that deck. Littering his life.

She.

The deepest cut, if he and Chris were right.

"What do you want to do about it?" Mel asked.

The cold night air swallowed Hawes's bitter chuckle. "You're gonna have to be more specific."

She laid a hand on his shoulder, squeezing, then nodded toward the other boat. "About that?"

The boat, the bodies, were evidence Chris and Kane and their teams could use. That maybe even Holt could extract valuable information out of. Hawes never put anything past his hacker twin.

"*Sell it,*" Chris's voice echoed in his head. Sell the story they needed her to believe.

She would want it destroyed, would want all the evidence erased. *Clean up your messes.* That's what she'd taught him.

"*Protect him,*" Chris had urged.

Hawes glanced over his shoulder at Wheeler. Burning the boat would accomplish that too. Would buy Hawes time to convince Wheeler to play along. To keep him safe. To fool her.

And that's what Hawes had to do. Fool her. Put on the best performance of his life. Because if he faltered, if he couldn't sell it, the lives of too many people, including those he loved, would be on the line. Hell, were already on the line. Losing them—losing any more innocent lives in the fallout—was unacceptable. It violated his rules. Rules he had fought too damn hard for, lost too damn much for, and he would be damned if he didn't see them to victory.

For the sake of his family, his heart, and his soul.

Sell it.

He righted his gaze and nodded. "We burn it."

Hawes flipped through the morning news programs. On one, the woman he recognized as Chris's boss, Special Agent in Charge Vivienne Tran, was claiming victory for last night's seizure of a major weapons cache. Kane stood beside her, looking grim and uncomfortable in his uniform. Another local station showed predawn footage of the smoldering salvage vessel. A third featured exterior shots of MCS's headquarters. Business as usual there this morning, except for the cops at the gate, checking anyone going in or out. Three flips through each program and no other references to his company, his family...or Chris. Or the unconscious agent in the infirmary bed beside which Hawes sat. Tran didn't mention any loss of life in her remarks, focusing instead on the weapons seizure and case closure, the successful culmination of a long-term ATF operation. No acknowledgment of Christopher Perri's or Isabella Constantine's roles in that effort.

A wave of sympathy rolled through Hawes—for Chris's mission, for the agent's devotion to his partner, and for the difference Isabella had made in Hawes's life. For the better, even if it had led to the present chaos. Inevitable, if Hawes was being honest with himself. Change didn't happen without resistance. The new would always run up against the old. That was the way of the world—in business, in politics, in life, and in families, including his own...if he was right.

"You owe me two bounties."

Hawes muted the wall-mounted television and shifted his attention to the woman standing in the doorway. "Reeves's mercs?"

Mel nodded. "The price on their heads was high, but honestly, I'm not too cut up about it. Saved me the hassle."

Hawes slumped in his chair. "But brought you more."

She sauntered into the room and lowered herself into

the chair on the other side of Wheeler's bed. "You know, I've watched you for years. I even considered recruiting you and your siblings into the FBI, but I sensed something different about you three. That maybe you'd be more valuable on the outside. When you came to me three years ago, torn up and ready to make a real change, and when Holt and Helena backed that play, I knew I had made the right decision."

"And now?"

"More sure than ever." Her dark eyes flickered to the TV, the press conference still going. "Just finish this, Hawes, and stop making life difficult for my family and friends."

"Christopher Perri one of those friends?"

The corners of her mouth tipped up, like she was fighting a smile. "He's what you needed, isn't he?"

One second, he was amused at her playing matchmaker. The next second, the full meaning of what she'd said sank in, and Hawes shot to the end of his chair. "You sent him to me?" He had thought it was Amelia who'd sent Chris the flash drive that had accelerated his appearance on the scene and in Hawes's life. There had been two folders on that drive. One full of pictures of Isabella's crime scene. The other with various surveillance shots of Hawes, a bull's-eye on each. Enough to pique the interest of the investigator with a personal stake in the case.

"Chris was already sniffing around," Mel said. "He's a good man, a good agent, and he was getting closer by the day. I wanted to make sure he ended up on the right side of this." She leaned forward and pinned Hawes with a look he was sure more than a few targets had been uncomfortably familiar with. Her husband too probably. The don't-argue-with-me-because-I-always-win stare-down. "With you."

He wouldn't argue *that* point. He liked having Chris on his side too, for multiple reasons—professional and personal—but there was a fact still nagging him. "How did you get into Holt's system?" They had been sure it was Amelia, who had a photographic memory and who had frequently positioned herself to spy on her hacker husband.

"She didn't," a voice said from the doorway. "I did."

Hawes didn't have to ask who the man standing in the doorway was. He wasn't Hawes's type—too clean-cut, too boy-next-door—but he was no doubt the handsomest, and tallest, man Hawes had ever seen. His wide, easy smile was as inviting and attractive in real life as it was on ESPN, as was his honeyed Southern accent. Thank fuck Chris wasn't here to see Hawes swoon. And thank fuck he was sitting down so Jameson "Whiskey" Walker didn't notice either.

Mel's bemused chuckle shook Hawes out of his starstruck daze. "Hawes Madigan, meet Jameson Walker. Jamie, meet Hawes."

Hawes started to stand, praying for steady legs, but Jamie waved him back down. "Don't get up on my account." He approached with an outstretched hand. "Nice to meet you, Hawes."

"Likewise. I think my brother would like to meet you

too," Hawes said, returning the handshake. "Maybe also kill you."

Jamie laughed. "Sucks being second best."

"Don't let Lauren hear you say that," Mel chimed in.

"Correction," Jamie said, still smiling, "third best." The handsome man's grin dimmed, however, as he withdrew a flash drive from his pocket. "There's a reason Holt got this to us."

"Amelia's backup?" Hawes asked, and Mel nodded. Despite what they'd told Chris, Holt had found it earlier in the week, in a hospital lockbox registered to one of Amelia's nurse mentors who had recently retired. But finding it had been only half the battle. And Holt, after beating his head against the desk for days, hadn't been able to win the other. He had told Hawes he needed an assist. "You cracked it?"

"She used one of my older, more obscure protocols." Jamie handed him the stick. "Messy but relatively simple. Holt was overthinking it. I've made the same mistake too."

Mel rose to her feet. "We all have." From the look on her face, Hawes knew she wasn't only talking about the flash drive encryption. "It wasn't just you and your siblings she had evidence on."

"Her boss?"

Mel's expression shifted from bleak to sympathetic, and Hawes had his answer. Yes, they'd overlooked—or more accurately, willfully ignored—a messy but simple explanation. Hawes stood. Time to stop ignoring the mess and clean it up. "Got something I can play this on?"

"There's a laptop set up in the Talley stateroom, just

down the hall," Jamie said. "It's the oldest of the videos. We didn't open the rest."

"Plausible deniability," Mel explained. "I saved the decryption key on the drive so Holt can open them."

Hand to his shoulder again, Mel stopped Hawes in the doorway. "You might want to wait for Holt and Helena. I can get them here."

Hawes shook his head and averted his gaze, unable to bear the empathy and pity any longer. "I can't risk them," he forced out around the lump in his throat. "Not until I confirm what I *think* is in that video and decide how to play this."

"Okay." She dropped her hand. "We'll be here if you need us."

"Thank you," Hawes said, to both of them. This was more than they had to, or should, do. But this—these connections with good, decent people, people who had his, Holt's, and Helena's backs in the midst of an epic shit-storm, allies he trusted—was what he had to fight for. A better way to conduct their business and their lives. One based on trust, cooperation, and respect, not on fear and betrayal.

Two unsteady steps later, he paused and called after Mel, "Is our mutual friend okay?" He didn't mention Chris by name, preserving Jamie's deniability, just in case.

"He's at SF General," she said. "Out of surgery and in recovery. Stable condition. Kane will keep us updated."

An ounce of steadiness returned, and Hawes let it carry him the rest of the way to the stateroom. He counted his steps and measured his breaths until he stood behind the desk, flash drive in hand and laptop open. If he didn't know the *Ellen* was dry-docked, he would have sworn it was at sea, being tossed around by a hurricane. He lowered himself into the chair before the storm in his head took out his limbs. No swooning this time, just abject terror and despair at what he was ninety-nine percent certain he was about to see.

He plugged the flash drive into the computer. It lit up, as did the dark screen, the icon for the drive highlighted. Hawes closed his eyes and tried to breathe around his racing heart. He picked up his counting again—breaths, pulse, the nicks in the desk on either side of the leather desk blotter. But the counting didn't calm him; it only seemed to compound his rising anxiety. He needed to get steady. He withdrew the burner phone from his pocket and punched in Chris's number. Thumb hovering over Send, he glanced out the window, across the Bay toward SF General. Would Chris even be awake to take his call? Would he curse Hawes for contacting him—the fed Hawes supposedly tried to kill? For not selling it? She would doubt his loyalty, and Hawes was already up against a mountain of suspicion.

She.

Fuck it.

Hawes tossed the phone on the desk, double-clicked the flash drive icon, found the single decrypted file, and in the drop-down menu, hit Open. A video window appeared —dark—with a prompt to hit Play.

He clicked—another second of darkness as the video loaded—then his world exploded.

He thought he was prepared for it, all but certain of what—*who*—he was going to see. He wasn't wrong as to the parties on-screen: Reeves, Amelia, and her. But he wasn't prepared. He wasn't ready for the explosion that rocketed through him.

He smashed the keys as he desperately tried to pause the video, to pause the truth so it didn't blind him all at once. The playback froze on a picture of her. Gray hair perfectly twisted into a chignon, Chanel suit perfectly in place, her facial expression perfectly imperious. Hawes slammed his eyes shut, a million denials running through his head despite the truth on the screen, the truth he and Chris had already put together.

Chris.

Hawes scrambled blindly for the phone. He clutched it in a death grip, as if he could draw some steadiness out of the mere possibility that he could call Chris or his siblings.

Fuck, his siblings. What was this going to do to Holt and Helena? They were already fraying at the seams, and now this. To learn that the last remaining pillar of their family…

Hawes lost the battle with the storm, his insides surrendering to the riot of thoughts in his head and the pain in his heart. He shoved back from the desk and grabbed the nearest trash can, spinning so he faced away from the computer and door as he emptied his stomach. It didn't relieve the sour in his soul or in his gut, and the sting and stench of bile in his throat and nostrils only made it worse. He had to get rid of it, had to not look at the computer screen again just yet.

Had to deny the truth a little longer.

He stumbled to the en-suite bathroom, washed out the trash can and his mouth, then, back in the main room, made a beeline for the wet bar, aiming to burn away the remnants of the awful taste in his mouth. He shuffled around bottles until he found a whiskey, one that cost far more than his Crown Royal, but it did the trick, giving him a different kind of burn than bile and betrayal to focus on. He tossed back the rest of his first pour, then poured another two fingers' worth into the cut-crystal tumbler. He started back toward the desk but only made it halfway, stalling out at the end of the bed. It didn't, however, stop the scene from the video replaying in his mind.

Disregarding the people in it, the setting was familiar to Hawes. From the plate-glass windows overlooking the Bay, to the fluted plaster crenellations around the door and the metal seismic struts running to the roof, to his brother's command station visible through a connecting door. They were in Hawes's office at MCS, formerly his grandfather's. And that's what the three people in the video had been arguing about before Hawes had paused it.

"*He's cutting me off,*" Reeves had said. "*Do you know how much this is going to cost me? This is not the agreement I had with Cal. We were supposed to do more business together, not less.*"

"*Have you talked to Hawes?*" Amelia asked.

"*He says MCS is going a different direction.*"

"*He is the CEO now.*"

"And the other business?" Reeves glared at the older woman behind the desk. *"It's not only official business I need the Madigans for. Cal understood that."*

"We expected some shifts," she answered. *"Some new ideas."*

"Do you expect his legacy—"

"He's not dead." The daggers of ice in each word were enough to cut, as were the daggers shot from the ice-blue eyes in her murderous expression.

That's where Hawes had managed to pause it. Where he needed to resume. Sitting on the end of this bed was not going to change what happened in the past. But facing the truth could change the future. He had to finish this—the video, and all of it. He downed the rest of the whiskey and stood. He grabbed the burner phone, clutched it tight, and situating himself in front of the computer again, pressed Play.

In the video, Reeves stepped back and raised his hands, palms out. "You're right. My apologies." He lowered his voice and continued, tone and manner deferential. "When he passes, will your family's empire survive? Because this isn't the way to do it. And I'm not the only one Hawes has cut off. You need to bring him in line."

"We're working on it."

"Why didn't you take over?"

"Because day-to-day operations has never been my role. And there are complications I'd rather not be tied to directly."

"Complications?"

"You likewise might be better off unconnected," Amelia said. "For the moment."

Reeves looked back and forth between them. "You've got a mole?"

"We're handling it," the other woman said. "And we'll handle Hawes."

A shiver ran down Hawes's spine, replaying how she'd handled him the past three years. The setup with Isabella, using him as a scapegoat. Conspiring with Jodie, Ray, and Lucas to kill him. With Amelia, Zoe, and Reeves to hijack the explosives. Going so far as to willingly injure herself. All to handle him.

"Rest assured, the ship will be righted, and you'll be there with us. With me." Her tone had melted from winter to spring, sweet enough to draw the bees into her garden. Like she had drawn so many people into her web over the years—business leaders, socialites, and politicians, all dirty enough to be leveraged. That's what she did best. That was her role. And she'd weaponized it against Hawes. "Can I count on your support?" she said to Reeves.

"Of course," he acquiesced, putty in her hands.

Because *she* was the queen. Because she was Rose Madigan, and Hawes had been a fool to forget his grandmother was the most dangerous of them all.

Hawes watched from the infirmary window as the late afternoon fog rolled back in, snaking around Sutro Tower and through the city's skyscrapers, creeping toward MCS and the waterfront, across the Bay from where Hawes was still waiting on Scotty Wheeler to wake up.

The holding pattern, while frustrating, had also been valuable. It had given him time to process and plan. He was still working out details—contingencies if Wheeler didn't cooperate, if Helena or Holt didn't get on board, if Rose didn't buy his performance—but he was more confident now than he had been last night or this morning. Granted, he still didn't have all the details—there were more files for Holt to decrypt—but Hawes had enough to go on.

He turned the flash drive end over end in his hand, started to clutch it like he had the burner phone, then stopped himself. The narrow piece of plastic wouldn't withstand the force, though even the phone hadn't withstood his anger. As soon as Hawes had been able to think straight after watching that video, he'd texted Holt: **Get Lily. She stays with you, Hena, or Brax at all times.** Immediately after, he'd powered off the device and hurled it against the wall, shattering it to pieces. The swell of anger, and its release, had felt good. He'd used that rolling wave to power through the rest of the day. Mel had checked on him periodically, bringing him food he forced down and updates about the investigation and Chris, who was still unconscious post-surgery. Chris's family was at the hospital, as was Hawes's. Hawes didn't necessarily like that Helena and Holt were in the same place, but at least Kane was there too, standing guard.

Now, if Wheeler would just wake up, Hawes could get

the rest of his plan underway. On cue, a groan sounded behind him. Hawes turned and waited with his back against the wall, watching Wheeler grow increasingly agitated, as if caught in a nightmare. Hawes knew the feeling well and was sure when he got the chance to sleep again, the memories of shooting Isabella would be joined by fresh ones of shooting Chris. Torture all the same, no matter if the latter had been done with permission.

Mumbling from Wheeler brought Hawes back to the present. The sounds resolved into a name. "Sam... Sam, no..."

"Wheeler." Hawes stepped toward the bed. "Wake up."

The agent's breath hitched, and his body froze, surprised into wakefulness. The next instant, he visibly forced his breathing to even out, pretending to still be asleep.

"I know you're awake, Scotty," Hawes said, trying the nickname for more of a response.

Nothing.

Hawes wasn't going to pry—he didn't like when strangers pried into his nightmares either—but Wheeler wasn't giving him a choice. He had to do something to break this standoff. "Who's Sam?"

Another hitched breath, and then dark blond lashes fluttered up, the brown eyes underneath hazy but alert. "I don't know any Sam."

Yes, he did, and Sam, whoever they were, haunted the man's thoughts. Sympathetic to his plight, and having gotten what he wanted, Hawes let it go. "All right."

"Where am I?" Wheeler asked.

"On a boat."

"Captain obvious," Mel said, appearing in the doorway. "You're on the *Ellen*, Agent Wheeler. Talley Enterprises' flagship vessel."

Wheeler's eyes rounded, wide as saucers. "Agent Cruz." He struggled to push himself upright and winced. Hawes moved closer to help, and Wheeler jerked in the opposite direction.

Judging by that instinctive reaction and the wariness in his eyes, Wheeler still read him as an enemy. Hawes mentally recalculated his contingencies; he might have to put the first into action right away.

Or he could wait and let Mel work her magic. "Just Ms. Cruz now." Smiling kindly, she approached Wheeler's other side and helped him into a less vulnerable position.

He relaxed a measure and split a glance between them. "What happened? How did I get here?"

"You were shot," Hawes said.

Wheeler laid a hand over his side, over the surgical gown that covered the bandaged gunshot wound Zoe had inflicted. "By one of your people."

Hawes shook his head, covering the fresh surge of betrayal that made him want to wince too. "Not one of mine."

"Hawes brought you here," Mel said. "Got you medical attention."

"Why did you do that?" Wheeler asked, eyes narrowed.

"Because that's what Chris wanted." Hawes lowered

himself into the chair he'd occupied for most of the past twenty-odd hours. Doing what Chris had asked. "He told me to protect you."

Lines formed in the agent's forehead. "You were working together?"

"Not exactly." Yes, they'd planned the strike together, but Chris had had another objective, which he'd then altered mid-course. They hadn't planned that part together, but it had worked out in Hawes's favor.

Wheeler tapped his thumbs against the bed rails, no doubt trying to sort out the tangled course of events. "But you are now?"

Hawes tilted his head. "Not exactly."

"So what, then?" Wheeler barked, growing impatient. Hawes had to admit, he kind of liked needling the agent. It was the first bit of amusement he'd had since... He couldn't remember. Wheeler, however, wasn't amused. "You're holding me hostage?"

"Technically, your agency thinks you're dead."

Saucer-eyes returned. "What?" Wheeler pushed back up, wincing but not stopping, until Mel put a hand on one shoulder and Hawes on the other. "I need a phone. I need to call—"

"Whoever you need to call," Hawes said, "if you want to keep them safe, if you want to see them again, you need to stay dead." He stepped back when Wheeler shrugged him off. "At least for a few days."

"And you expect me to trust you?"

"Chris did."

"Not a ringing endorsement," Wheeler said. "He's a wildcard. The whole agency knows it."

"You got on board with his plan yesterday."

"Because he's also one of the best agents I've ever worked with."

"I feel the same," Mel said. "And if that's not enough, then trust me."

As Wheeler considered that, Hawes played his ace, or what he hoped was his ace, while they had the opening. "I need you to take this to Chris." He held out the flash drive. "He needs to get it to Holt, who can finish the decryption. It's a copy of Amelia's backup."

"You had it all along?"

"We didn't know who we could trust either. Now I'm trusting you."

Wheeler took the flash drive, handling it as if it were a grenade. Smart man. "What's on it?"

Hawes tried not to shatter the bed rail where he gripped it, the anger lapping at the shores of his control again. "Evidence that my own grandmother has spent the past few years trying to overthrow me."

Wheeler's gaze shot to Hawes, but he didn't look surprised. Chris had mentioned that he had Wheeler digging into Rose. This was the other reason Hawes had needed him to wake up.

Hawes reclaimed his chair, crossed one knee over the other, and clasped his hands in his lap, ready for whatever revelations Scotty Wheeler was about to unload on him. "What else did you find out?"

Wheeler's gaze flickered to Mel, and at her nod, back

to Hawes. "She has a separate trust set up for Lily. But you all have trusts set up for Lily, so I didn't think anything was odd about it. Until..."

"Until what?"

"I found trails of communication between Rose and former Madigan clients, including Carl Reeves."

"Did you check her travel and communications against Jodie's and Ray's? Against Lucas's and Zoe's?" The dead lieutenants who'd betrayed him. Hawes suspected they'd find her visiting the same coastal motel when Jodie, Ray, Lucas, and Amelia had. That she would have taken more meetings with Lucas and Zoe, probably at the off-site warehouse where the explosives had been stored. And stolen from.

"That search was running when I left for the op last night."

"Get those results"—he nodded at the flash drive in Wheeler's hands—"and that to Chris."

"How?" Wheeler asked, the confused expression back on his face. "You just said I'm supposed to be dead."

"Don't get seen." Hawes withdrew a folded slip of paper from inside his coat pocket and slid to the end of his chair. "Then go here to hide out after." He'd called in a favor from Shawn Gillespie, who, in return for Hawes having gotten, ironically, this particular ATF agent off his back, was more than happy to offer up one of his real estate projects as a safe house. "Don't tell anyone you're going there."

Wheeler gave the note a cursory glance, then folded it around the flash drive. "Why can't you take this to him?"

Hawes rested his elbows on his knees. "Because I have to go convince my grandmother I've seen the error of my ways."

"You're going in?" Mel said from across Wheeler's bed.

"There are answers we still don't have. Answers Chris and I, and the rest of my family, need. Inside is the only way to get those answers."

"How will you convince her?" Wheeler asked.

"I burned Gilbert's salvage vessel last night. I'll tell her you were on it. That I destroyed all the evidence against her. That and the fact I shot Chris should buy us a few days."

"You shot—"

"He's fine." Mel's hand on Wheeler's shoulder kept the agent from rocketing up again and doing more damage.

"But the ATF—"

"Has accomplished its primary objective," Hawes said, "according to your boss's press conference this morning. The explosives are secured. No mention of you or Chris, by the way."

"She plays things close to the vest," Wheeler said. "She was out for you and your family too. We can't be sure she's going to drop it."

"All I need is a few days to try and save what's left of my family, my organization, and my city." Hawes rose and stood at Wheeler's bedside, not bothering to hide the plea from his voice or eyes. "Will you help me?"

"Why me? Why not Cruz?"

"Because trust is a two-way street." That's what he and Chris had failed to realize until it was almost too late.

What his grandmother failed to realize was in their family's best interest going forward. Trusting Wheeler now would hopefully be further proof that Hawes's way forward was the better one. "Chris said to trust you. Now you need proof of my motive. So I'm trusting you."

"He said you were different." Wheeler closed his fingers around the piece of paper and flash drive and nodded. "Don't make him a liar."

CHAPTER TWO

Chris sensed eyes on him, multiple sets. Combined with the furious keystrokes and repetitive beeping, Chris felt like he was in an action movie, like there was a metronome counting each beat of rising tension. Counting down to some suspenseful event. He doubted opening his eyes would be all that exciting. Especially not when he was lying flat on his back in a hospital bed, judging by the beeping heart monitor, the lingering antiseptic smell, and the post-surgery ache in his shoulder. He opened his eyes, and, as expected, the sight of generic, white ceiling tiles was less than earth shattering. The relative dimness of the room, however, was curious. Had he beat the morning sun? He must have been rescued quickly. He'd seen the flare hit the water above him, and now here he was, alive, with sensation in all his limbs, including the arm pinned to his chest in a sling. Had they rushed him from the scene directly into surgery?

He rotated his head to the right, guessing the direction

of the window based on the fading cone of light on the ceiling.

Celia's tired yet relieved face cut off his view. "Hey there," she said.

Cee, he tried to return, but his mouth was too dry.

Beside Celia, a second person appeared, her blonde hair atop her head in a messy bun. "Drink, Mr. Hair," Helena said, holding out a paper cup. Celia propped the pillows behind him, and Chris pushed himself up with his good arm. He took the offered cup and sipped through the straw, slurping loudly in the otherwise silent room.

Silence.

The typing had stopped.

And with that realization came another that made Chris's pulse jump.

Lily. He'd last seen her with...

The worry must have shown on his face because Helena's fell to match. Chris's heart skipped another beat. Until she lifted her gaze to the opposite side of the bed. Chris whipped his head around, faster than he should have—twin spikes of pain and nausea assaulting him—but at least his heart resumed its regular rhythm. The redheaded munchkin was safely tucked in a sling against her father's chest. The sight was comforting enough to even ignore the Toronto Raptors T-shirt Holt wore beneath his flannel.

"Hawes texted," Helena said. "After all that's happened, we're not in the habit of questioning him."

Chris took another gulp of water, then handed the cup back to Helena. "I need you to remember that."

"What's that supposed to mean?"

Chris eyed the woman beside her, and Celia scoffed. "I know that look," she said. "Shop talk, and not my kind." She lifted a hand, fingers spread. "Five minutes, for Mom and the kids to see you. They've been waiting all day."

"All day?"

"It's almost eight."

"In the morning?"

"At night."

"You've been out all day," Helena said. "Doc said your body was demanding sleep."

"Fuck sleep." He moved to sit fully upright, ignoring the pain that shot through his shoulder. They had to get out of here, find out what Hawes needed, how they could help him. "We've got to—"

Helena planted a hand on his chest. "You know I can take you healthy. I can fuck you up good like this." Her evil grin left no doubt as to the truth of that statement. "Doctor and family first."

"We don't have time—"

"It'll give us time to call Brax back from the cafeteria and to get Rose here."

Chris swallowed back a wave of nausea. "Just Kane."

The siblings exchanged a look, and the air in the room grew heavy, ripe with tension. As did Helena's hand still on his chest. Had they already discussed the possibility? Or did Holt and Helena still doubt his loyalty? The latter would be fair; he couldn't blame them. Either way, they let it pass for now. Holt nodded, and Helena removed her hand, after a little shove. "Always a negotiation with this one."

"Try growing up with him." Celia rolled her eyes for added effect, and the tension in the room eased.

And eased further with the parade of visitors that followed. The doctor on duty checked his wound—a clean through and through, no damage; Hawes had known exactly where to aim—and pronounced him healing well. Dischargeable by the end of the night, thank fuck. After the doctor left, Gloria barreled in with a box of mistletoe cannoli, Mia with a paperback for him, and Marco with eyes that kept straying to Helena.

"Too old for you, Plato," Chris said, and his nephew turned beet red as the rest of the room erupted into laughter.

Helena bumped his shoulder. "Don't take it personally. I only date folks older than me." Her blue eyes strayed to Celia, who was older than her by three months.

Chris did not want to think about that. Better to think about another cannoli instead. They demolished the box of pastries, leaving only one for Kane, who, when he entered the room, moved to stand behind Holt and Lily. The chief made polite chatter, but his attention was mostly on Holt, who hadn't spoken other than to settle his daughter or mumble, "Thank you," when handed a cannoli.

Once his family finally cleared out, and it was just Helena, Holt, and Kane in the room with him, Chris asked, "How did you get the visiting hours relaxed?"

A pale Holt finally spoke. "They're used to us around here. Amelia..."

Chris could have kicked himself. Of course. Holt's wife had been a nurse here. The whole lot of Madigans were probably fixtures here too. They certainly had been over the past two weeks.

"All right," Helena said, taking up position on the windowsill. "Spill, Mr. Hair."

"Where's Rose?" he asked.

"At MCS, I assume. She's been holding things down there." Helena crossed her arms. "You didn't want her here."

"What's this about?" Kane asked.

There was no easy way to do this. Just rip off the Band-Aid. They didn't have time to waste. "We think she's the traitor."

Helena shot forward, bearing down on him. "*We?*"

"Me and Hawes, I think."

She stopped at the bed rail, barely. "You think?"

"We didn't get to work it all out, given the circumstances. I wanted to be sure before leveling that on him."

"But you'll level it on us? You could just be trying to tear this family apart. More than you already have."

So maybe that earlier tension had been about him, then, not Rose. "If you don't trust me, why are you here?"

"Because you had my back last night." Her gaze flickered to the door. "And your sister is kinda hot."

"Fucking hell." Chris scrubbed a hand over his face. "That's the last thing any of us need right now."

"I'm not good enough for your sister?"

"No, that's not it at all." He dropped his hand. "You're exactly what she needs, but after the bullets stop flying, please."

Helena shrugged. And fought a smile, poorly. "Fair enough."

"What proof do you have?" Kane asked, bringing them back on track.

Chris began counting off on his fingers. "She's the person with the juice to make this happen. The Madigan with the most connections." He lifted a second finger. "She and Cal built this empire, your parents fueled the fear and image of a killing machine, and now Rose doesn't like where your generation"—he split a glance between Holt and Helena—"is taking things." A third finger. "She's all about power. I saw that Wednesday night at the Buena Vista. She's intimidating as hell."

"Speculation based on circumstantial evidence," Helena said.

"Lawyer."

"Yes, that's my day job, remember?"

"And yet you"—Chris shifted his gaze to Holt—"don't look surprised."

The oldest Madigan in the room remained tight-lipped, and the tension ratcheted up again. Until Lily's soft snuffles turned into a wail, and everyone's attention momentarily shifted to taking care of the littlest Madigan. Helena fetched a bottle out of the diaper bag, and when Holt lifted Lily toward Kane, the chief took her and the bottle. He situated the munchkin in his arms and began feeding her like it was the most natural thing in the world. The surprising sight would have kept Chris transfixed, if not for Holt retrieving the laptop he'd set aside and turning it so the screen faced Helena and Chris.

"Reeves wasn't on Rose's list," Holt started, voice scratchy. "When he showed up at MCS last night, her omission was hard to ignore. I've been digging to see when and where their paths last crossed."

"Anything?"

"Almost all their contact went through Amelia." He pointed at the windows open on the screen. "Phone records, email records, and several reservations and other meetings. Same time and place."

"You said *almost*."

"There are instances of them at the same events, around town and whatnot. And he was a veteran too, so he was at those benefits with us."

"What else?" Helena asked, accurately reading her brother's caginess.

He turned the computer halfway back around, closing windows and opening others. "I also went back and looked at visitor logs."

Kane peered over his shoulder. "Are those for the hospice house where Cal—"

Nausea walloped Chris again, and Helena looked sick to match. "He was there?" she asked, voice barely a whisper.

Holt nodded, and Helena inhaled sharply, her knuckles white where her hands curled around the bed rail. Chris laid his good hand over one of hers and asked the question she couldn't. A question no kid or grandkid should have to ask, but that's where they were, and Chris hated Rose for putting them—and him—in this situation. "Did she have anything—"

"No," Holt said, and Helena exhaled her held breath. "I contacted the doctors. She had nothing to do with Papa Cal's death. Completely natural causes."

"But Reeves was there," Helena said, "plotting with her and Amelia to kill our brother."

"They were plotting it long before then," came a voice from the doorway.

If not for the Georgia-twang on the last word, Chris wouldn't have recognized the man dressed in Talley Enterprises coveralls, his face shadowed by a Giants baseball cap, beads of sweat at his temples. Scotty Wheeler leaned precariously against the door jamb, and his feverish brown gaze darted around the room, settling, to Chris's surprise, on Holt. The plastic stick he held up explained the direction of his focus. "I have proof, from your brother."

"Which one is that?" Kane griped gruffly, despite the nursing baby in his arms. "I'm getting tired of fucking flash drives."

Chris shared the sentiment, except there was a certain flash drive still at-large that held special interest for him. He had a feeling he was looking at it in Wheeler's hand. "Is that—"

"Amelia's backup," he confirmed.

Helena withdrew her hand from under Chris's before he could crush it. He tried crushing her with his scowl instead. "You had it all along?"

"Didn't trust you. Still don't completely." She shifted her icy glare to Scotty. "Trust you even less. What are you doing *here*, with *that*?"

"As I said, your brother gave it to me." He glanced

nervously over his shoulder, back toward the hallway. "And I'm supposed to be playing dead, so..."

"Get in here, Scotty," Chris said with a wave.

Wheeler hobbled forward and collapsed into the chair on the other side of Helena. Once Kane moved in front of the door, Wheeler removed the ball cap, revealing sweat-soaked hair, and unzipped the coveralls partway, exposing a gray T-shirt that was likewise damp in places. He did not look good, and the hand he placed over his side, right where Zoe had shot him, did not make Chris feel any better about his condition.

He nudged the pitcher of water on the bedside table. "Get him some water," he said to Helena. He didn't want Wheeler to pass out before he divulged what had happened to Hawes. Chris had kept those worries at bay long enough to reassure his family, and to prepare Hawes's for the worst, but now he needed to know Hawes was okay.

Helena beat him to it. "How's Hawes?" She held a cup out to Wheeler, who took it and drank greedily, until Helena *tsk*ed at him. "Easy, or you'll throw it all back up."

Wheeler finished more slowly, then handed the cup back to her. "Your brother's not at all what I thought."

"Great, you're having an epiphany, but how—"

"I suspect it's been one of the worst days of his life."

Chris bit out a curse. He'd fucking slept the day away *here* while Hawes had been out *there*, somewhere, dealing with God only knew what, alone. Chris should have been there. Should have gone with him last night. "Fuck," he cursed again.

"That flash drive have something to do with it?" Helena asked.

Wheeler dropped the device into her outstretched hand. "You need to be prepared for what you're about to see."

"I briefed them in advance," Chris said. "About Rose."

"You were right to have me look into her."

Helena tossed the flash drive across the bed to Holt. "Cue it up, Little H." She was putting on a front for Wheeler, acting casual and unaffected, like she was unbothered and in control, but Chris had seen that control slip a moment ago, and he didn't miss how the wobble of her hand threw off what should have been a practiced toss.

Holt nevertheless caught the drive without issue. He plugged it in, then adjusted the laptop so it was visible to the room again.

"I'm going to step out," Kane said.

He made it less than a step before Holt shot out a hand and grasped his elbow. "I need you to stay."

Kane motioned with his arms, Lily still in them, toward Helena. "I can give her to—"

"You," Holt rumbled.

Wheeler watched the exchange like it was a tennis match, Chris like it was further evidence to support his suspicions, and Helena like it was a day that ended in Y. Holt and Brax, for their part, seemed to forget anyone else was in the room.

"I've got earplugs," Holt said, "if you need them."

Chris took pity on them. "There are two federal agents in this room. Plausible deniability is off the table."

Denial, however, was the emotion that invaded the room once they'd watched the video. Sitting on the arm of Wheeler's chair, Helena stared into space and clicked her nails together, a nervous tendency akin to Hawes's counting. By the window, Holt stood holding Lily, giving his head a shake every few seconds. Chin ducked, Kane waited by the door, arms crossed over his chest, keeping one eye on the floor, the other on Holt. Even Wheeler looked stunned.

For his part, Chris had absorbed all of Helena's earlier anger and was ready to explode with the force of it. Ready to rocket out of this bed, out of this hospital, so he could hunt down Rose Madigan and exact justice for what she'd done to the family in this room, to Hawes, and to Isabella. He was sure that's who Rose and Amelia were referring to in the video. Promising to "handle" both Izzy and Hawes. Setting the one up to die, the other to die or take the fall.

But Chris couldn't leave and couldn't do a damn thing about his anger because of the damn IV in his hand, the ex-soldier blocking the door, and the missing Madigan who had embarked on a dangerous solo mission. Exactly as Chris had told him to do. He fell back on his pillows and stared at the ceiling. It was the right call—fuck, the only call—and he'd suspected this much, but having it confirmed, knowing with certainty what Hawes was walking into, made his gut clench with fear for him.

"What are we going to do about this?" Helena asked after another minute of silence. Past her denial, then; she'd skipped right over the other stages of grief to acceptance and planning.

Impressive.

"Hawes is already doing something," Chris said, righting himself. "He's going back in."

Holt spun from the window. "He's *what?*"

"I told Hawes to sell it." He pointed at the gunshot wound to his shoulder. "I told him to shoot me, to protect Scotty, and to sell it. He's going to bend the knee."

Anger roaring back, Helena grabbed the paperback Mia had left on the table and chucked it at him. "This is not a fucking fantasy novel."

He batted the book down, and it landed in his lap. "In a way, it is."

"Why would she trust him?" Kane asked.

"He shot me. By all appearances, he killed Scotty. He wielded a gun for the first time in three years. He'll pretend to abandon his other rules too, pretend to be the soulless assassin she wants him to be, so he can get inside and get the evidence we need."

"You're still after what happened to Isabella," Helena said.

"For what happened to my partner *and* your brother. Neither of them should have been put in that situation."

"And the ATF will play ball?" Kane asked Wheeler.

"I can't say. I'm dead." He curled his fingers in air quotes around the last word. "But that"—he nodded at the laptop—"is evidence your grandmother was the genesis of the current case. We get more evidence to prove that, then yes, I think the ATF will focus on Rose."

"Why are you helping us now?" Helena asked.

"Your brother could have let me die last night, but he

didn't. And you have friends"—he tapped the TE patch on the coveralls—"who I trust and respect. They believe you're truly trying to make a difference. I may not agree with your approach, but in this case, we're on the same side." Wheeler was proving the faith Chris had put in him had not been misplaced. He'd admitted his mistake last week, realigned his approach to the case and the Madigans, and now they had another resource and friend.

"Glad you came to see that," Chris said.

He sheepishly shrugged a shoulder. "Turns out we should have been trying to slay the queen."

"And who's going to worry about Hawes?" Holt asked from where he sat propped on the windowsill. "Who's going to pull him back if he has to break his rules?"

"Me," Chris said without hesitation. "I'll pull him back."

"Why?" Helena pressed.

"Not gonna tell you," he said, "before I get to tell him, properly." *I think* wasn't good enough. Chris was pretty damn sure he *knew*, if his earlier anger and the ache in his chest were any indication. And he was damn sure Hawes would be the first to hear *those* words.

One corner of Helena's mouth tipped up. She knew the answer. He figured they all did. "How's that gonna work with you being ATF?"

"I won't be, after this is done."

Various expressions of shock filled the room, except from Kane, who already knew Chris's intentions. Wheeler's surprise faded first, the agent no doubt putting together the pieces. So Chris spoke to the two Madigans who still needed convincing. "I want a life and home with Hawes." Either at Hawes's condo or at his, and regardless of location, he knew who would be showing up, unannounced, to interrupt them, frequently. "And God help me, I want all of you to be a part of that future, with us."

CHAPTER THREE

"Are you done trying to kill me?"

The chair behind Hawes's desk swiveled, its occupant rotating to face him. In the otherwise dark office, the twinkling lights of the bridge, combined with the moon's reflection off the water, cast Rose Madigan in an eerie, foreboding glow. One Hawes had only ever associated with Papa Cal, one that others likely associated with Hawes, but in that moment, his grandmother wore it better than either of them ever had.

"Are you done disrespecting your grandfather's memory?" Rose countered, not bothering to deny the truth of Hawes's question. Her verbal knives were almost as sharp as her icy glare. "Your parents'?"

"That's not—"

She tapped at the in-desk controls, and the room lights came on. "They built all of this," she said, gesturing at their surroundings. "And our other empire. Both were running smoothly, thriving, until you started severing relationships.

Started turning down work, making unwise alliances, and crusading for justice." She spat the last word like a curse. "What was wrong with the way they—*we*—did things?"

Life, work, companies had to evolve. *They* had to evolve. To keep up with technology, with the criminal landscape, and with the new and better tools law enforcement had to navigate their world. And *he* had to evolve. His conscience demanded it—demanded justice—ever since the night he shot a supposedly innocent woman.

He didn't say any of those things to his grandmother.

"I was taking steps to insulate us from the law."

"And now they're closer than ever."

She wasn't wrong, though the attention from law enforcement had started long before his ascension. Hawes remembered his parents' many absences, Cal and Rose's too, the closest scrutiny coming when Noah and Charlotte had died. Lying low, hiding from enemies and the law after particularly high-profile jobs, one of which had killed his parents. They operated an organization of assassins; attention from the law would always follow them. But it didn't have to be the kind they ran and hid from, and they didn't have to engage in side businesses—like manufacturing and trafficking explosives—that attracted even more attention. He would not put his niece and any future niblings, or if he was lucky enough, his own children, in the situation he and his siblings had been in as teens. Of being alone when they needed their family most. And yes, law enforcement was closer than ever—with Chris and Kane inside their circle, and Mel and her connections a phone call away. They were inside, yes, but working with them. Making their city safer. Crusading, maybe. Surviving, definitely.

He didn't say any of that to his grandmother either.

"I recognize my errors," he said instead, twisting deeper those knives she'd thrown. "I acknowledge them, they're mine, which is why I'm here. To clean up my mess, and I need your help to do that."

"I don't trust you," she said.

"I don't trust you either." No sense beating around that bush. And no sense appealing to familial ties; that was clearly a nonstarter, given her inference of disrespect. Deference, then. "But I'll answer your questions truthfully, here and now. And then maybe we can negotiate a way forward." He gestured to the visitor's chair. "May I?"

The blue-on-blue stare-down lasted ten long seconds before Rose nodded. His ass had barely hit the seat when the inquisition began.

"Where have you been the past twenty-four hours?"

"There was the small matter of evidence to destroy."

"I saw the news," she said. "No one mentioned any bodies being found on board the salvage vessel."

"Probably because they're still trying to identify them."

"How many?"

"Six." Lie one. "Reeves, Gilbert, Zoe, two mercs, and the fed."

"Which one?"

"ATF agent Scott Wheeler."

"The other fed lived?"

Hawes kept his face blank as he pulled Chris's service weapon from the holster nestled uncomfortably under his arm. He'd swung by his condo before coming here, for a shower and a change of clothes, and to dig the shoulder holster out of the bottom of his closet. After three years, carrying again felt unnatural, as had the several times he'd handled this particular weapon over the past two weeks. It was a relief to get it off him and lay it in the center of the desk. "I shot him, with his own gun, and he fell overboard into the Bay. That's the last time I saw him."

Rose flicked her gaze to the gun, then back up to him. Granted, she could pick it up and shoot him at any second, but she would have done that already if she was going to. "He doesn't seem to want to die," she said. "He's at SF General, recovering from surgery."

Hawes slid back in his chair and crossed one leg over the other. "I didn't intend for him to live." Lie two.

"And if I asked you to take that gun and kill him? For good this time?" She said it casually, as if asking him to do a small favor for her. Not like she was asking him to snuff out the flame that had burned through him the past two weeks, hot and bright. To kill the promise of what that heat might spark where there had been so little warmth for years.

"I would, if that's what it takes to win back your trust." Lie three. "Though I think that's an unwise move. He's too visible."

"He won't stop until he learns what happened to Isabelle."

"What did happen to Isabella?"

Finally, a flinch. Because he'd used the undercover agent's real name that Chris had drilled into him? Or because there was more there? "It's the past," she said. "We need to move on."

Not so fast. "I thought you wanted me to respect the past?"

"Yes, respect our decision on how that particular matter was handled."

There was that word: *handled*. Hawes wanted to rail. He didn't do that either, because there was definitely more there, which made the lies and restraint worth it. "He no longer has jurisdiction," Hawes said. "I saw the coverage too. The ATF seized the explosives and closed the case. His boss, SAC Tran, said so in the press conference. If Perri persists, we report him, and he'll be out of our hair."

"That's been taken care of already."

Hawes forced himself not to lurch forward in his chair. "Tran's in your pocket?"

No answer.

Fuck, the last thing Chris needed was someone inside his own agency gunning for him too. How had Rose gotten to an ATF SAC? How long ago? "Have you known what the ATF was up to all along?"

"No one was watching while *I* kept tabs. While *I* kept this family and its legacy as the number-one priority." Fire burned in her eyes, and a small smile turned up the corners of her mouth. Too reminiscent of Helena's when she had her target right where she wanted them.

A full-body chill raised the hairs on Hawes's arms. He waited for it to pass before speaking, not wanting his voice to waver. "You have to give us that information, if we're to continue to carry on the legacy."

"I gave it to one of you. The one I trusted implicitly."

"Amelia."

"You want to prove your loyalty to me and to this family? Get Amelia back."

"We've gotten her the best attorney—"

She reached out and pushed the gun back toward him, her eyes piercing and determined. "That will take too long."

Hawes eyed the gun warily as he struggled to wrap his brain around the gauntlet that had been laid in front of him. This sort of extraction was not in their usual job description. "You want me to break her out?"

"I need her for the next phase." With her manicured nails, Rose traced the edge of the framed photo of Lily that Hawes kept on his desk. "And Lily needs to visit with her mother."

Hawes didn't disagree, though the implication that Holt wasn't enough rankled. As did the implication that Holt would somehow deprive Amelia of contact with Lily, even while Amelia was in prison. What rankled most, though, was Hawes's certainty that Rose's motive for getting Amelia back had more to do with needing her to hack something—again, lack of confidence in Holt—than with Lily's well-being.

"How do I know she won't kill me the instant I free her? That my death or my siblings' isn't a part of your next phase?"

"She has her orders. And you're going to have to trust me." When her gaze cut to the gun again, Hawes read the silent order and retrieved the weapon, securing it back in his holster. "You are my grandson. My blood. I love you. I don't want to kill you, or Holt, or Helena. But I will do what I have to to get this family and our businesses back on track. To see that Cal's, Noah's, and Charlotte's contributions don't go disrespected or wasted. We retain our power and protect it for future generations. That's how the Madigans survive and prosper."

Power, by force and might. Same as Amelia had argued. And what did power respect? More power. She'd perceived him as weak, so she hadn't respected his rule. He'd have to show power to earn back her respect and trust and to fool her into believing he'd returned to the fold. And then he'd give her a goddamn coup.

But there still had to be an escape route for the innocents. Her affection for Lily, he hoped, would make her amenable. "A show of trust, in return?"

Her eyes narrowed. "What do you want?"

"No harm comes to Kane."

"I thought you recognized and acknowledged your errors."

"I'm not asking for myself or because Brax is a cop. I understand that was an ill-conceived alliance. I'm asking because we've kept one member of this family relatively clean, and if anything happens to the rest of us, he's going to need his best friend to help him pick up the pieces. For Lily."

"That dependency—"

"Is something none of us can understand. We didn't live through what they did." While Holt had never told them exactly what had happened in his last year of service,

Hawes was certain his twin wouldn't have survived at all if not for Braxton Kane.

Rose folded her hands in her lap. "All right. And in any event, if he becomes a problem, I can have his badge with a phone call."

"Just don't take his life."

"And you'll free Amelia?"

Hawes stood and buttoned his coat, as satisfied as he could be negotiating his life and those of his loved ones with his own grandmother. "I'll make it happen."

Hawes held it together long enough to make it to his condo. Just barely. He closed the door, activated the security locks, and flipped on the hallway lights. Propped against the foyer pole, he toed off his shoes and tilted back his head, staring at the ceiling and counting—wires, track lighting, sprinkler heads. Anything to calm the rapid breaths that had started in the Lyft. Once they'd crossed King, on their way to his place in South Beach, some part of his brain had judged him far enough away from MCS and his grandmother to begin to unravel.

And now the threads were slipping faster, while the pressure on his chest mounted, like a landslide of rocks burying him, making it hard for his lungs to expand and take in air. Pushing off the pole, he shed his coat and ripped out of the shoulder harness, tossing both at the loft stairs. He loosened his shirt buttons and staggered toward the open living area, toward more air.

Iris greeted him at the dining table, winding around his ankles. The weight on his chest eased a measure as he knelt and ran his fingers through her silky black coat. She *meowed* pitifully. "I know, girl. I'm sorry I haven't been around much. It'll get better soon, I promise."

She blinked her big yellow eyes at him, then, as if judging him a liar, she turned tail and scaled furnishings and cabinets, disappearing over the half wall to his lofted bedroom. Someone else he'd let down. Someone else whose trust he had to win back. Add her to the list. A list that was about to get even longer.

His windpipe constricted as more boulders piled on, stealing his breath and balance, forcing him to brace his hands on the table. He dug his nails into the weathered wood and willed steadiness and control back into his being. Didn't work. Frustrated at the weakness in his limbs, at his lack of control over this whole goddamn situation, at the losses suffered and those likely still to come, he lashed out, sweeping an arm across the table. A stack of cookbooks, a paperback, a water glass, and a leftover coffee mug tumbled to the floor, the latter two shattering.

He stole a breath. Finally.

Desperate for another, Hawes spun and searched for his next target. Desk. He kicked the rolling chair out of the way, then cleared the desktop with two satisfying passes of his arm. Papers, pens, and other home office detritus clattered to the floor.

Breathing came a little easier.

He uncuffed his sleeves, rolled them up, then launched himself over the couch. He flipped over the coffee table, sending a vase and remotes flying, on his way to tearing apart the media unit. By the time he was done, vinyl records, more books, and two broken game controllers littered the floor.

But he could breathe. Lungs finally full, almost to bursting, he ripped off his shirt and braced his hip against the panic room ladder, sucking in giant gulps of air and expelling them in choked huffs. Just this side of sobs. He closed his stinging eyes, saw his grandmother's cold blue ones in his mind, and when his windpipe constricted again, he shifted to kick the ladder. And only managed to hurt his foot, the ladder locked into place on its short track. But the pain was good. It provided a point of focus other than the knives still lodged in his heart, twisting and tearing him apart every time he remembered Rose's words. Her accusations. Her expectations.

Fuck, he needed something stronger than the twinge of pain in his foot. He bypassed the liquor cabinet, wanting cold oblivion tonight rather than the burn of whiskey. On his way to the kitchen, he kicked the closest metal barstool at the island, and the line of them toppled over, the crash loud and satisfying, dampening her words that played on repeat. The cool, crisp Pilsner he grabbed from the fridge, and drained, muted them further.

But it did nothing to mute the very real voice that came from overhead. "Feel better now?"

The empty bottle slipped through Hawes's fingers and would have shattered on the floor if he hadn't slowed its momentum with his foot. Hawes bobbled the bottle with his toe, nudged it toward the recycling bin, then lifted his gaze, and lifted it more, to the man whose head and torso appeared over the loft wall above the kitchen. The very last person who should be here. "What the fuck are you doing here?" he snapped at Special Agent Christopher Perri.

Not that he wasn't happy to see him. He was happy and so fucking relieved—Chris was here, alive and breathing, his brown eyes alert and his long hair tied up in a messy topknot—but the two of them spending time together, here at Hawes's condo, was possibly the most dangerous thing either of them could do right now.

"Thought you might need to let go," Chris said. His gaze wandered past Hawes, to the open area behind him. "Did a fine job of that yourself."

Hawes looked over his shoulder at the mess he'd made... The mess... He shook away the nagging conversation with Rose and focused on the mess here. His eyes tracked to the far end of his unit, to the giant glass windows and balcony doors there. "If someone saw you or heard you..."

"We're clean for bugs."

Hawes opened his mouth to remind Chris of the clever bug he'd planted here a week ago, but the agent beat him to it.

"I even checked Iris," he said. "And no one saw me. I kept it dark, then came up here to stay out of sight." He nodded toward the windows, and hair escaped his wobbly bun. "And because lying down is easier on this." He cringed as he shrugged his bandaged shoulder, ignoring the sling that was clearly supposed to keep it stable and still.

Breathing became difficult again. "Fuck, I'm so—"

"I told you to shoot me. Did it work?"

"Maybe. I don't know." Resting back against the island, Hawes curled his fingers over its edge. He closed his eyes and hung his head, reality heavy as fuck again. "My own—"

"We'll talk about that after."

Hawes blinked and lifted his head. "After?"

"Get up here, Madigan."

His small inviting smile made Hawes's stomach flip, in a good way. Made Hawes want to sprint down the hallway and up the stairs to the loft. He forced himself to do the opposite. To pick up the beer bottle, wash it out, and toss it into the recycling bin. To right the barstools. To grab his coat and gun holster off the stairs, to hang up the first and secure the latter in the closet safe, before finally taking the closet-side stairs one at a time up to the loft.

Chris, in jeans and nothing else, was waiting in the center of the bed, stretched out with Iris on his bare belly, scratching her behind her ears. Maybe she hadn't been abandoning him earlier but rather returning to her new favorite human. Hawes would be jealous if not for Chris's heated gaze tracking his every step as he moved to the side of the bed.

"I'm a little offended it took you so long to get up here."

Hawes reached out and pushed back a strand of hair that had fallen across Chris's face. "I was trying not to seem desperate." He lingered there, tangling his fingers in the hair at Chris's temple.

Chris's gaze raked down his body to the erection tenting Hawes's slacks. So much for not seeming desperate. Smile wicked, Chris shooed Iris off his lap and off the bed. Sitting up, he swung his legs around to hang on either side of Hawes's. His molten gaze burned back up Hawes's body, as did his right hand, up the back of Hawes's thigh and over his ass, kneading a cheek possessively. "You desperate, Madigan?"

Stepping forward, Hawes wove both hands into Chris's hair, loosening the hair tie so the strands fell loose through his fingers. He cupped the back of Chris's head, tilted his face up, and stared into his dark eyes as relief pushed balance and steadiness back into him. So much relief. Chris was here, alive, and he was letting Hawes touch him like this, after everything. "More desperate than you know," he said, voice rough with need. "But we should talk. So much has—"

"We'll talk, but I don't think that's what either of us needs right now." Hand tightening on Hawes's ass, Chris drew him closer and nuzzled his belly. "And I know about desperate." He opened his mouth, and warm breath seared Hawes's skin. "Fuck, baby, I know."

Hawes's stomach more than flipped, and his right hand did a fine imitation of its somersaulting, flitting above Chris's left shoulder. "But your injury."

Chris captured his hand and pressed it lightly against the bandages. "This," he said, then using Hawes's hand in his, pulled Hawes onto the bed with him, and once they were stretched out, dragged Hawes's hand down to his crotch. "Has nothing to do with this."

Hawes curved his fingers over Chris's dick, stroking it through the denim. Hard as Hawes's, and from the groan that rumbled out of Chris, aching just as badly. "Are you—"

Chris surged up, cutting him off with a kiss that silenced anything and everything but Hawes's need to be with him. His need to taste every corner of Chris's mouth, to bury his nose in the crook of his neck and inhale the scent of eucalyptus, to feel every inch of his body against—inside—his own.

Need that was reflected in Chris's words when they next broke for air. "I'm sure I need to be back inside you as fast as I can get there." Chris lifted his right hand and cupped Hawes's cheek. "As long as you're sure too. But if you need to talk now, we will."

Hawes muffled his strangled, bitter laugh in Chris's palm. He was the one who'd murdered Chris's partner, he was the one who'd lied time and again this past week, he was the one who'd shot him, and yet, Chris was here, in his bed, hard with want and handling him with care. If there was no doubt in Chris's mind, there was certainly none in Hawes's. He'd gotten over any doubt about where Chris's heart lay during the night they'd shared at Chris's place, and over any doubt about his allegiance last night when Chris had shielded him from flying bullets. Hawes's heart and mind were in the same place—with Chris.

He kissed Chris's palm, then reached across him to the bedside table and retrieved a condom and lube from the drawer. "I'm good with after." Rising on his knees, he finished undressing them, and once stripped, rolled the condom down Chris's dick. Chris shivered under him and bucked as Hawes stroked his erection, covering it in lube.

Then Hawes reached behind to ready himself. "What's easiest?" he asked on a panted breath as he worked himself open. "With your shoulder."

Red streaked across Chris's cheekbones as he eyed Hawes hungrily. "Ride me. Unless you need more, and then I'll make it work."

He would always need more, but he understood what Chris was asking. If he needed Chris to exert more control so Hawes could let go, he'd find a way. Like he'd been doing the past two weeks. Tonight, though, there was only one thing Hawes needed. Ready, he snagged Chris's hand and brought it to his hip. "Keep me steady."

Chris fanned his fingers over skin and bone and squeezed. Hard. "Always."

Hawes covered the weightlessness that overwhelmed his insides by bringing his weight down on Chris, slowly sinking onto his cock. "Dante," tumbled from his lips, and Chris groaned, his fingers digging into Hawes's hip. Chris's sling-trapped hand splayed on his own chest, scrabbling for purchase, and Hawes reached down to tangle their fingers together. He reached his other arm over Chris's head, grasping the headboard, then rammed back down onto Chris's dick.

"Fuck yeah," Chris cursed, grip tightening in both places he held him. "Let go for me, baby."

And Hawes did, filling himself over and over with Chris, the taste of his mouth and skin, the scent of his sweat and sex, the thick fullness inside him, deep inside him, and the lightness it brought to every other part of him.

Both lost and found in the fog of lust—and love—that wrapped tightly around them.

He dragged his mouth over Chris's scruff-covered jaw, to his ear. "I don't just think," he said between grunts, the speed and force of their thrusts violent almost, their orgasms near. "I know, Dante."

Chris lifted his hand off Hawes's hip, and Hawes cried out from the loss, until Chris brought the hand to his cheek. Handling him so gently while his cock pounded inside him, pegging his prostate with unerring accuracy. He ran a thumb over Hawes's cheekbone, drawing his gaze. Hawes saw the same flood of emotions reflected there, then heard it in Chris's wrecked voice. "I know too."

And after that there was nothing left to see. Hawes's orgasm barreled into him, blinding him to everything but the gentle hand on his face and the strong, hard body climaxing beneath him, the man who was lost in pleasure—and love—with him.

CHAPTER FOUR

"I'm not sure this is the best thing for your gunshot wound."

Chris tightened his good arm around Hawes's bare chest and kissed the shoulder freckle he'd been worrying with his teeth. "That's why I'm sitting behind you"—he tapped his foot against Hawes's at the far end of the soaking tub, splashing the shallow water—"with my bandaged shoulder wrapped in towels and my upper half out of the water."

Hawes had left the bed to toss the condom and get them washcloths, and Chris, remembering a certain fantasy he had involving this tub, had followed him down the loft stairs to the bathroom. Approaching from behind, he'd snuck a hand over Hawes's hip and down to his dick, teasing and tempting as he'd made his demand for a bath known. Hawes had conceded, as had Chris, allowing the turban of towels around his bandaged shoulder.

Hawes lolled his head on Chris's other shoulder and

nipped at the underside of his jaw. "You gonna do more than just tease?"

Chris trailed his hand down Hawes's lean, chiseled torso, under the warm water, and circled Hawes's cock, giving it a tug and relishing the quake of the body in his arms. Thanking all that was holy for the chance to be here again with Hawes Madigan. Touching, teasing, together.

"Eventually," he said. While Hawes was seemingly ready to go again, Chris's recovering body needed more time, and his brain needed to fill in some blanks from the past twenty-four hours. One more stroke, then he withdrew his hand, chuckling when Hawes muffled a whine in his neck. "I promise," Chris assured him, looping his arm back around Hawes's chest, holding him lightly. "But first, we need to talk."

"So this was a trap," Hawes said, even as he closed his eyes and relaxed into Chris's embrace.

Ridiculously pleased at that sign of trust, at the small victory in an otherwise raging war, Chris hid his smile in the divot of Hawes's collarbone. He swirled his tongue in the groove, and Hawes squirmed, stretching like a cat seeking more. He spread his legs, stiff cock breaching the water's surface, and Chris, his own dick reawakened, reconsidered whether they really needed to talk first. But then Hawes righted his gaze and tensed, seeing something Chris didn't.

Chris drew back and nuzzled behind his ear. "What is it?"

Hawes lifted a long leg out of the water, and with his

big toe, traced the tile sun framing the faucet. "This was one of the last things he remembered how to do."

Chris didn't have to ask who Hawes was referring to. All he had to do was look around the bathroom, at the yellow and white tiles that brightened the otherwise enclosed space. At odds with the condo's sleek modern design, the tile work had obviously been done after Hawes had bought the place. By a master...or his apprentice; by a king...or the prince. A touch of home, of family, that Hawes had brought with him. "Papa Cal helped you lay this?"

"No, but he told me how." Hawes inhaled sharply. "Asked about it every time I visited." Another short, shaky breath. "He didn't always remember who I was, but he remembered I was the one laying tile in a bathroom." His breathing grew ragged, like before when he'd torn apart the living area.

It had torn Chris apart to wait in the loft while Hawes had let go without him. But Hawes had needed that then, and Chris would have been no help with his own anger and bum shoulder. Now, though, unwound, Chris could help cushion Hawes's landing as he suffered the hard fall back to reality. Chris pressed his chest snugly against Hawes's back. "Breathe with me," he said. "In." He inhaled, lifting his chest and relaxing his arm as Hawes's chest expanded. "And exhale." He deflated back to neutral, his hold steady but light.

In and out, together, until Hawes's breathing returned to normal and he slumped back into Chris's body. "Thank you."

Chris kissed his temple. "Time for that talk."

Nodding, Hawes curled his hands over Chris's forearm, holding him there. "You saw the video?"

"Scotty brought it to us."

A big relieved sigh. "Good, he made it to you."

"Barely," Chris said. "But yeah, he got there. We got him an IV before he left again. Said you'd arranged a safe house."

"One of Gillespie's properties down on the Peninsula."

"Fitting bit of irony."

Hawes tilted his head and flashed him a smirk. "I thought so."

"Thank you for keeping your word and protecting him."

"Thank you for trusting me," Hawes said, before his contented expression was replaced with a pained one. His voice was strained to match. "Fuck, Chris, my own grandmother."

"I'm sorry I wasn't with you when you had to watch that." Holt and Helena had taken it hard, and they weren't the ones who'd been directly targeted, the ones Reeves had directly blamed, the ones Rose had promised to "handle." Chris couldn't imagine what Hawes had gone through watching that truth unfold, digesting it alone. Chris's chest ached, and he held Hawes tighter.

"Puked," Hawes said, "then washed my mouth out with fifty-dollar-a-glass whiskey." He moved out of Chris's arms but only to run a splash of hot water and wet a washcloth. "I came by here after, showered and changed, then headed to MCS."

"Earlier, you said you weren't sure it worked."

"Neither of us trusts the other, and she's so fucking cryptic. Always has been." He scooped water into the rag and scrubbed his face. "I suspect she bought it as much as I buy that she won't try to kill me again. Or use me as a fall guy if things go sideways."

Chris removed the rag from his hands and set it on the ledge. He shifted Hawes between his legs, as much as the tub allowed, and curled a hand around his neck, turning his face to him. Pale skin red from the hot water and emotion, the ends of his light brown hair wet, his blue eyes damp with sorrow, Hawes looked far removed from the thirty-three-year-old king of corporate and criminal empires. "You don't have to do this," Chris said. "We can find another way."

Hawes shook his head, drops of water falling from his hair onto the back of Chris's hand. "That's time we don't have." Determination shoved aside the misery in his eyes. "And I don't want to be on the outside. Not if she's trying to get her hands on those explosives again. I can't risk what she might do with them. Or what she might do, period."

"You think that's what she's after? The explosives?"

"She wants me to break out Amelia." He fiddled with the towels around Chris's shoulder. "Given their obsession with power, I'd guess the explosives are involved somehow. There's the sheer power of them, plus the message it'll send, if they can steal them back from the ATF."

Chris shook his head in frustration and dismay. "Quiet power is far more frightening."

"I agree. Case in point, Helena, who strikes silently but is deadly. We don't need the explosives, or the guns for that matter, but that's not how Rose sees it. I'm hoping she's so blinded by her need for loud power that I can get to Amelia and leverage her."

"For?"

"The truth about Isabella." Hands flat on Chris's chest, Hawes had to feel Chris's galloping heart. Hawes's was likewise working overtime, pulse hammering under Chris's hand around his neck. "Was there anything else on the flash drive?" Hawes asked. "About her?"

"Holt was still decrypting files when I left, but he didn't think so. There was evidence to implicate all of you, like Amelia had said, but nothing else about Izzy. You think Amelia knows more?"

Hawes shifted forward, ran another splash of hot water, then rested back against Chris's chest. "She's been Rose's right hand this entire time. Maybe Papa Cal's too. She was in that video with Rose and Reeves from years ago, and it had to be Isabella they were talking about. If she made one video, then..."

"Stands to reason she made more." Chris snagged the washrag and soap and began skimming them over Hawes's torso in a light wash. "I can deputize you. Transfer her into your custody."

"I'm not supposed to be working with you."

"And Tran would probably never go for it."

Hawes laid a hand over his, stalling its motion. "We need to be cautious. Rose said something that made me think Tran could be dirty."

"For real? Or was Rose playing you?"

"Either way, it's worth looking into. And worth our

caution." He released Chris's hand, and as Chris resumed the light scrubbing, he rested his head back on Chris's shoulder. "We don't know the full scope of Rose's reach."

"All right, I'll get Scotty digging into it first thing. And we'll proceed with caution. What else do you need?"

"Get a message to Holt and Helena. They need to appear to fall in line, but behind the scenes, Helena should rally the captains for when we're ready to make a play."

"I'll haul them into the station for more questioning. Or make it look like that." Chris smiled, despite the complicated maneuvers they were discussing, despite all the complications this conversation was bringing up. Because despite everything, it felt good, natural, being here at home with Hawes and strategizing with him. Like partners.

"What's that grin about?" Hawes asked, looking up at him.

That only made him smile wider as he pushed a damp flyaway off Hawes's forehead. "I like working with you, not against you."

"Me too." Hawes nipped at the underside of his jaw, but then grew quiet. His hard swallow echoed in the silence, and Chris cuffed his neck in comfort, as if he could steady the words for Hawes, make them come easier. They did, after a moment. "There's something else," he said. "I need you to help me minimize collateral damage. That's off the table for me now."

No, there was no *easier* way to deliver those words. The pain they brought was evidenced in Hawes's strangled voice and in the way Chris's insides knotted in sympathy. "Hawes..."

Blue eyes blinked up at him, pleading. "Help me make it so it doesn't reach the table at all. I have to be able to come back from this."

Chris drew up his left knee, forcing Hawes to turn into his chest and allowing Chris to wrap his right arm more fully around him, nestling him in. He dipped his chin and rested his forehead against Hawes's. "No matter what, I will wait for you on the other side of the fog."

"Why?" Hawes whispered against his lips. "I killed your partner."

Chris opened his mouth to say what had been swirling in his head during the strike at MCS, and later, what had crystallized as he'd lain there in that hospital room.

But Hawes beat him to it. "We have to talk about that too," he said, starting to draw back. "Until last night, I thought you were going to kill me."

Chris halted his retreat, hand palming the side of his face and drawing him back in. "I know you." He kissed one sharp cheekbone. "I know you love your family, all of them, even the ones who betrayed you." Kissed the other. "I know what you are and what you want your organization to be." Kissed the crease that formed between his brows. "You could have pulled that trigger against me the morning I revealed myself, but you didn't." Kissed the tip of his nose, and then his lips, lightly. "You wouldn't, just like I know, given the choice, you wouldn't have killed Isabella that night either."

"I'm sorry, I didn't—"

"I know now you didn't mean to kill her."

Hawes covered his hand with his own, leaning back enough to lock their gazes. "I want justice for her too. Everything I've done since that night has been about righting that wrong."

"I know that." Chris slipped his hand out and kissed Hawes's palm. "I'm sorry I almost destroyed your family to figure that out."

"We were all played. Everything I did... It wasn't enough." He closed his eyes, defeat stealing over his features again.

Chris could commiserate. The same weariness infused his bones from driving himself into the ground, and driving his family away, these past three years. Hell, the past ten. But over the past couple of weeks, he'd seen the path back from that dark place to a renewed closeness with his family and a home with the man in his arms. If they were going to get there, though, he needed to resurrect the man who'd time and again walked into a trap and turned it around on the fool who'd thought him weak. The strongest man Chris had ever met, who'd turned Chris's world upside down, for the better.

His king.

"Listen to me, Madigan." He gritted through the pain of pulling his arm out of the towel sling, because dammit, he needed two hands for this. He framed Hawes's face, holding his gaze, his attention, their world, steady. "The organization needs you. Your family needs you. I fucking need you."

"Why?" Hawes choked out.

"Because I don't just think I'm falling for you. I fell, baby, the minute I walked into Danko and saw you across the room, your head held high like you fucking owned the place. The second you called me Mr. Perry." He gave him a little shake for emphasis. "*I know.*"

Hawes closed his eyes, and Chris's heart skipped a beat, until they opened again, full of resolve. Of that same confidence he'd fallen for. "I fell for you that night I walked into my condo and saw the box of mooncakes. You got it. You got me. *I know too.*"

"Then we'll get her," Chris said, heart racing now, with love and hope for the future. "And we'll get justice for Isabella, for our families, and for us."

"And then?"

"And then we'll rebuild the empire, by your rules, better and stronger than ever before. Together."

The king smiled—wicked, deadly, and fucking glorious.

CHAPTER FIVE

Chris grabbed a cold pack out of his mom's freezer and laid it atop the assortment of foodstuffs he'd tossed into the cooler. Snacks for Mia and Marco on the drive up, everything his mom and sister needed to make the family lasagna once they reached their destination, and a bottle of wine for all the trouble Chris was causing them.

He zipped up the cooler and carried it to the dining table, where Mia glanced up from her e-reader. "Is this really necessary?" Despite her griping, Chris's niece was ready to go, her bookbag and duffel on the floor by her feet, while the rest of the family was still upstairs packing.

"Are you really complaining about a week in Tahoe?"

She shrugged a shoulder, insolent teenager in full effect.

"Let me guess," Chris said. "This has to do with the guy."

"Ethan," she supplied. "And no. Aunt Ang was

supposed to teach me the mistletoe cannoli recipe this week."

"Fuck, Mia," Chris said, genuinely apologetic. "I'm sorry to make you miss that."

"Language," Celia said as she crossed the family room toward them. She dropped Marco's duffel next to Mia's, then kissed the crown of her daughter's head. "And I'll teach it to you this week at the cabin."

Gasping, Mia swiveled in her chair. "You've known this entire time?"

Celia shrugged, and Chris laughed at the similarities between mother and daughter. His smile lingered at seeing the spark back in Celia's eyes. He hated asking his sister to drop everything at the shop, and likewise interrupting Gloria's, Mia's, and Marco's lives, but he needed them safe, which meant far away from the shit going down here. At least Celia had a solid garage staff to cover for her, and the kids would get a nice midsummer vacation on the lake. Chris wished, more than a little, that he could join them. Maybe also bring—

"Chris, grab the cannoli ingredients and add them to the cooler," Celia said, snapping him out of his daydream.

Mia whirled back around, glaring at him. "You too, Baelish? Traitors, the whole fucking lot of you."

"Language!" Celia chided again, but the accompanying laughter belied her scolding. "I'm going back up to herd the others."

She disappeared up the stairs while Chris made several trips to the fridge and pantry, gathering cannoli ingredients and adding them to the cooler. "We're all taught the recipe, right around your age. But there's usually only one in a generation with the patience to make them."

"I can't wait to learn," Mia said, eager in a way she wasn't about most things at her age. "I've got the muffins down and the cookies too. Cannoli would be an awesome way to end the summer."

Chris figured he knew who'd be second in command at AB's before long. More immediately, though, there was another piece of family history he needed Mia to protect. From his saddlebag, he retrieved the weathered Sendak book which had been his daughter's, Rochelle's, favorite.

"Why do you have that with you?" Mia asked.

He lowered himself into the chair next to her. "I need you to keep it safe for me."

Worry overtook her expressive features—dark brows drawn, the darker eyes beneath them wide, her upper teeth worrying her bottom lip. "Why's it not safe at your place?"

He opened the book to the picture of Ro tucked between two pages. "I'm probably being overly cautious." His condo was between two other units in a three-story Mission Dolores Edwardian. A property-destroying attack was unlikely, but he couldn't be sure with the way things were escalating. And he had to be sure with this. "I can't let anything happen to this piece of her." He closed the book, picture tucked safely back inside, and held it out to Mia, who'd been Ro's biggest fan and best friend. "Can you do that for me?"

Eyes glassy, Mia took the book and tucked it into her bag.

"Thank you," he said, extending his good arm for

a hug.

She tipped sideways into him. "Thank you for trusting me with it."

Trust went hand in hand with family, or it should have. Chris couldn't help but think of Hawes and the betrayals of trust he'd suffered lately. His grandmother, Amelia, his lieutenants, Chris.

Chris hoped he'd done enough last night to convince Hawes he could be trusted, but Hawes would still be within his rights not to trust him. And vice versa. But at least they were moving toward the same goal. Hawes and Rose weren't, which Chris feared would undermine any trust the one was pretending to have in the other. Which would in turn lead to God only knew what kind of chaos in the coming days.

A series of *thunks* on the stairs drew Chris out of his thoughts and up from the table, hurrying over to help Celia with the suitcases. "We're about ready," she said. "Lake Tahoe, here we come."

"How *did* you magically make a cabin in Tahoe appear?" Mia asked.

Chris tossed his badge onto the table with a grin.

"Didn't your mom teach you not to lie, Mr. Hair?"

Chris glanced over his shoulder to find Helena, dressed in riding leathers, strutting across the parlor, arm in arm with his mother.

"Of course I did," Gloria said. "Can I get you a coffee, dear?"

"That'd be lovely, thank you."

Chris waited until Gloria was out of earshot before

murmuring, "Way to invade my family."

Helena shoved her helmet at him and shook out her hair. "You invaded mine first."

Celia snorted. "Nice to see someone throwing it back at him for a change."

"Hey!" Chris protested, but neither woman seemed to notice him.

"You have something to do with this impromptu trip to Tahoe?" Celia asked Helena.

"My brother, but I'm gonna make sure you get out of town safely."

Celia's blush knocked five years off her thirty, until the flirtatious grin fell from her face and she turned fretful eyes to Chris. "Are you—"

"I'll be fine, Cee."

Gloria rejoined them and handed a steaming mug to Helena. Her words, however, were for Chris. "We just got you back."

"And I'm not going away again that easily," he told the three Perri women staring at him with the same skeptical eyes.

"Mom!"

Saved by the screaming preteen upstairs.

"Duty calls," Celia said, then to Helena, "Hold him to that."

"Count on it."

Celia nudged Mia up from the table, beckoning her to help Gloria take the first load of luggage down to Celia's SUV in the garage.

"You shouldn't be here," Chris said, once it was just

him and Helena in the room.

"No one saw me."

He set her helmet on the table. "You don't think anyone will see you escorting them out of town?"

"If anyone sees anything, it'll look like I'm tailing them." She sipped from the mug, then judging it worthy, gulped less cautiously. "Do you trust anyone else to do it?"

Of course he didn't. "Thank you."

"You need to focus." She finished her coffee and moved to the kitchen to wash out the mug. "And they need to be safe for that."

He leaned a hip against the counter next to her. "Well, this does save me the hassle of hauling you and Holt into the station."

"Why were we coming to the station?"

"It was supposed to look like we're cutting ties."

"As a front for what?"

"Planning Amelia's jailbreak. Hawes met with Rose last night. She demanded a show of loyalty and her right hand back in play."

"Fuck." Her confident nonchalance disappeared, and she braced both hands on the counter, shoulders hiked and head hung between them. Loose blonde strands hid her expression, but Chris could guess at it well enough. He covered her hand closest to his, as he'd done before at the hospital, giving her quiet support as she gathered herself. She kept things buttoned up, same as Hawes, but where his control manifested as chilly and untouchable to outsiders, Helena played the family spitfire, strategically aiming all that fire in the courtroom or in dark alleys. Or in a well-timed caustic barb. Which made these quiet moments even more stunning, same as the woman.

She inhaled deeply, relaxed her shoulders, and lifted her head. "How is he?"

"Better." Chris tossed her a goodwill match. "After I spent the night with him."

She scoffed and rolled her eyes, and when they righted, he was glad for the mischief and gratitude sparking in them again. "Thank you for being there for him."

"He needs all of us now."

"How does he want us to play this?"

"How do *you* want to play this?" Chris knew Hawes's plan, but it wasn't a bad idea to solicit a tactical perspective from the deadliest of the Madigan assassins and the person who spent her days testing the limits of judge and jury. She was a master tactician in her own right. Chris also wanted to see if the siblings were on the same page.

"We need to look like we're falling in line. Like Rose's takeover succeeded. At the same time, we work behind the scenes on a takeover of our own. Turn this whole shitshow back around on her."

Confirmation of Hawes's strategy and of the sibling synergy Chris admired, at least with respect to Hawes and Helena. But as to Holt... "Your other brother feel that way?"

"Let's find out." Helena withdrew a phone from her pocket and laid it on the counter.

A call was connected to a number Chris didn't recognize. The voice, however, he did. "I'm onboard," Holt said. "Helena can rally the captains."

Chris shifted his gaze between the phone and Helena. "He's been listening the entire time?"

"Yes," Holt said, "and Helena will give you the encrypted burner I sent with her as long as you shut up about your night with Hawes."

"Seconded." Helena dug another phone out of her other pocket and handed it to Chris. "You're both assuming I can rally the captains."

"Listen," Chris said, clasping her shoulder. "While it was your brother I fell for—"

"Oho," Helena said, brow cocked. "You're saying it now?"

Frustration and amusement warred. "Can I please finish paying you a compliment?"

Her manicured brow lowered, and the opposite corner of her mouth hitched up. "Proceed."

"You are damn impressive, Helena Madigan." He gave her shoulder a squeeze. "*That's* why Rose wanted to recruit you. The rest of the shit Reeves said—"

"Is true." Her gaze flitted to the garage stairs.

"Hena," Holt said gently. "What Reeves said has nothing to do with why the captains haven't broken ranks. *You've* kept them in line because *you* inspire loyalty. They'll continue to stand behind you."

She smiled softly. "Thanks, Little H." Then she tightened her jaw as she returned her attention to Chris. "Is that what Big H wants too?"

Didn't matter. "Is that what *you* want?" Chris asked instead.

"Yes," she answered without hesitation. "The rules

Hawes put in place have made us better. We need to keep going in that direction."

He was relieved she recognized that. Now she just needed to recognize in herself what everyone else did. "Then use your power to make sure they, and all of us, survive."

———————

Chris checked the rearview mirror for the umpteenth time in forty minutes. He didn't spot any tails other than the motorcycle several car lengths back. While Chris knew the bike was there, the casual observer wouldn't think anything of it. Just another vehicle on the road. The rider did a good job blending in. Not as good as Chris would have done if he were on his bike, but good enough to make Chris jealous. With one arm still in a sling, he wasn't about to risk the Hog, so he'd borrowed his mom's CR-V for this quick errand out of the city.

Another mile south and his exit appeared. Chris signaled to exit the freeway, without his tail. The motorcycle would continue on ahead, down 280 to the next exit, as they'd arranged. Following the map Hawes had drawn, Chris wound along Skyline for a few miles, crossed the intersection with Highway 92, then veered onto Cañada Road. As the Crystal Springs Reservoir glimmered to his right, he rolled down the windows and let the warm afternoon air inside, thawing him out from the city fog he'd left behind. He rounded a bend between two marshes, and then, as cypress trees rose on either side of the road, he came upon two weathered driveway posts. Chris turned onto the gravel drive, which sloped down toward the water. At the bottom of the hill, on the shore of the man-made lake, he came upon a collection of Cape Cod style buildings—cedar shake siding, pitched gabled roofs, and huge picture windows—all in various states of renovation. He parked in front of the largest of the three structures and was unloading tote bags from the trunk when the front door opened.

Chris almost dropped the bags. "I didn't think you owned any denim."

"Not mine," a dressed-down Scotty Wheeler replied. "There was a stack of clothing and first-aid supplies waiting for me when I arrived." He plucked at the untucked hem of the Gravity Craft Brewery tee he wore with a pair of Levi's. And no shoes. "Fits well enough."

"Casual looks good on you," Chris said, even if the rest of Wheeler looked rough. Wheeler was a pale guy to begin with, but the near-translucent pallor of his skin was worrisome. As were the dark circles under his bloodshot eyes. Chris reached the top of the porch steps, next to where Wheeler stood leaning against a post. "How you doing, Scotty, for real? Hiding out and playing dead isn't worth it if you actually end up dead." Collateral damage was collateral damage, and Chris wouldn't let Wheeler fall into that category with Izzy.

"Thanks, I think," Wheeler said with a half smile. "And I'll manage. It's more lack of sleep than anything. It's too quiet here at night. No bugs making a racket, and way the fuck out here, no city noise either. I was up all night,

jumping any time the windows or floors creaked, and—"
He cut himself off and ran a hand down his weary face.
"And now I'm rambling because tired and too much coffee.
Sorry."

Chris grinned, concern banked in favor of amusement.
"You know your Southern accent gets thicker when you're
tired and rambly?"

"I'm aware." He sounded as annoyed at himself as he
was at Chris for mentioning it. Chris chuckled, and
Wheeler gave up being perturbed. Smiling, he nodded at
the sling. "How about you?"

"It's more of a hindrance than anything." Like not
being able to ride his bike and not having two hands to
juggle the tote bags, which he lifted again one-handed.
"Let's get these inside. Groceries."

"You didn't need to do that," Wheeler said, holding the
front door open. "The clothes fairy stocked the fridge and
pantry too, though there was a shocking amount of
Dunkin' Donuts. If they weren't so damn good, I'd be
offended on behalf of LEOs everywhere."

Before Chris could inform him that it was likely the
local FBI ASAC who'd delivered the clothes and food,
they were interrupted by the crunch of gravel and rumble
of an engine. The motorcycle that had been tailing Chris
pulled into the drive behind the CR-V.

"What's this?" Scotty asked.

"Something else you need," Chris said with a wink.
The driver dismounted, removed their helmet, and ran a
hand through their platinum Mohawk, fluffing it back to
life. "You remember Jax?"

"Agent Wheeler," the IT specialist greeted. "Glad to see you're not dead."

"Scotty, please," Wheeler said. "And thank you."

"You mind some company?" they asked. "Agent Perri said you might need some help."

"With the investigation," Chris added, before Wheeler could object, correctly, to Chris's ulterior motive, namely not wanting Wheeler recovering out here alone. "No such thing as too many hackers."

Jax waited at the bottom of the steps, two saddlebags in hand. "And I make good coffee."

Wheeler narrowed his eyes at Chris, onto the truth, but his smile for Jax was grateful and polite. "I'd be happy for the help and the coffee. But fair warning, this place is spooky as fuck."

Wheeler wasn't lying. Once they got everything inside and unpacked, and Jax was setting up their computer workstation at the half-finished kitchen bar, Chris surveyed the large open floor plan. With most of the sparse furnishings covered in sheets, the new mantle above the stone fireplace bare and unstained, and no blinds on the still-stickered plate-glass windows, he got the spooky-as-fuck vibe all right, even in the middle of the afternoon. It was eerily quiet, eerily desolate, and eerily half-finished.

Chris swept his gaze from the sunken living room to the raised dining area, and to the long, wooden table covered in files and papers. "You've been working?" he said to Wheeler.

"Like I said, it's fucking spooky here. Can't sleep."

From what Chris had seen last week, the man didn't

sleep much to start with. "What have you got?" Chris asked as he circled the table.

"Based on my conversations with you and Hawes, I'm focusing my efforts in two places." Standing across from Chris at the middle of the table, Wheeler stretched an arm out to the right. "Connecting Rose to current events, namely the explosives and the related incidents over the past couple of weeks." Then to the left. "And connecting her to past events, including the night Agent Constantine was killed."

Not died; *killed*. Chris nodded at Wheeler for that acknowledgment, then moved toward the collection of evidence on present events. He spied a receipt for a private air charter, from San Francisco to Monterey, the closest airport to the remote coastal inn where the lieutenants who had betrayed Hawes had met and plotted the coup. "The dates line up?" Chris asked.

Wheeler nodded and handed him a copy of a page from the mayor of Monterey's official calendar. "She was on the mayor's agenda that day to discuss a fundraiser for Alzheimer's research. I called to verify the meeting. Rose cancelled at the last minute."

"Because she never intended to go. She was only using it as cover." He noticed a highlighted phone record next and slid it closer. "Rose's call log?"

"Yes. As I mentioned, she's been in contact with ex-Madigan clients. Those are the top three. Reeves, the Neo-Nazi who died in the sting last week, and Elliot Brewster."

Jax gasped. "The Madigans worked with that asshole?"

"He was the first person Hawes cut off when he

assumed control."

"And one of the first people to reach out to Rose." Chris tapped at the earliest highlighted entry, only a few weeks after Cal stepped down and Hawes took over.

Chris wasn't surprised that Hawes had cut Brewster off, or that Brewster had tried to use Rose to get back in the Madigans' good graces. He was a dealmaker, legit and otherwise. He fronted as a commodities trader, but in reality, weapons were his most profitable items of trade. He'd been on the ATF's radar for years. He also had a bad habit of treating women like objects to be traded too. He was presently on wife number four and had twice been accused of domestic violence. No charges either time, of course. It was almost as if he used the news generated from those incidents to cover his other illegal dealings. He hadn't been mentioned in any of Izzy's files, but that just meant he was more careful than Reeves. Or that Callum and Rose shielded contact with him particularly well.

"The arms dealer that was killed in the sting," Chris said, "was he affiliated with Brewster?"

"A competitor, from what I can tell."

"Hawes said he had contracts on each of them."

Wheeler pulled a bank ledger toward them. "Paid for by this entity." He pointed at a highlighted entry. A generic holding company name Chris didn't recognize. Didn't mean it wasn't connected to Brewster. Or Rose. "I didn't get very far before hitting a privacy wall."

"I can help with that," Jax said.

"Keep digging," Chris said. "This could be our way in. If it traces back to Rose, see where else her money goes, and comes from. She can't have funded all of this with Madigan money or else Hawes would have noticed. We need an independent money trail."

Chris strolled to the other end of the table, to the collection of crime scene photos and case files he knew all too well. And yet, had only just gotten a fuller picture of. "I can fill in more details about this night."

By the time he was done, Jax was silent, and Wheeler had collapsed into a chair, his elbows propped on the table, his head held in his hands. "How are you... How can you... Aren't you angry at—"

"I'm fucking furious," Chris bit out, letting loose a little of the anger he'd kept locked down. "And that anger almost cost you your life and almost cost me my family and my future." He shuffled papers and yanked out Izzy's ATF headshot. "It almost cost us any chance of getting her justice." He took a deep breath, reined the anger back in, and laid the picture down. "Because my anger was focused in the wrong direction. Hawes isn't the problem. Rose is the culprit. Hawes was just trying to protect his family, his company, and his city. He thought he was acting in self-defense. And maybe he was. We still don't know what happened during those few days before Izzy's death. She went dark. Amelia and Zoe both implied there's more to this." He turned his attention to Jax. "Can you help with that too?"

"I'll do what I can."

"Thank you." Chris stepped back from the table. "And make sure he also gets some sleep."

"I'm a hacker, Agent Perri," they said. "Not the best at

that either."

"Take shifts, then," Chris said, turning for the door. "And check in regularly."

Wheeler followed him out onto the porch. "You still don't trust me."

Nothing could be further from the truth. "Why do you think that?"

"Because you're not telling me everything." Despite the increasing paleness of his skin and the sweat dripping down his temples, Wheeler stood tall, demanding to be taken seriously.

Chris pointed back at the door, toward the table full of evidence the agent had already assembled, even operating at half-strength. "That case you're building in there is the key to shutting this down, once and for all, and getting justice for Izzy. You are the best agent I've worked with when it comes to the details, which makes you the best person for this task. Hawes and I need your focus here. Trust us that we're covering the other bases."

Wheeler held his stare one beat, two beats, then deflated. He rested back on the patio rail, head hung. "I'm sorry. I'm just not used to this."

"Used to what?"

"Someone wanting me on their team."

Chris clasped his bicep. "We do, Scotty. Don't forget that."

"Thanks." He cleared his throat, then lifted his head again. His gaze bounced around, landing anywhere but on Chris. "Listen, um, has the agency made any official announcement...about me?"

"Still listed as MIA. No official statement."

Wheeler tapped his thumbs against the rail, the rhythm rapid and irregular.

"Is there someone—"

"No," Wheeler cut him off. "Perri—"

"I think you can call me Chris."

"Chris, this job is all I have." His wandering gaze drifted back toward the house. Toward his work. "I don't want to lose it."

"Just trust me a little longer."

"We at least need to brief Tran, before she makes any further statements."

Chris looked away then. "About that..."

"Fuck, did Rose get to her too?"

"Hawes thinks it's possible. Add her to your dig list."

Wheeler ran a shaky hand through his dirty-blond hair, mussing it up more than it already was, the unstyled strands longer than Chris had realized. Despite the circumstances, casual and disheveled was a good look on Scotty Wheeler. "How big is this, Chris?" Wheeler asked. "When's it going to end? *How's* it going to end?"

"With us getting justice for our colleague and making this city a safer place." Chris had to believe that, on both counts, given the number of people depending on him. And if he and Hawes were to have any hope for that future —that home—Chris wanted. "That's our job, isn't it?"

"But is it going to get us killed?"

Chris sure as fuck hoped not, but he couldn't answer *no* with any certainty.

CHAPTER SIX

Blue eyes blazing, Helena squared off across the dining table from Hawes, every sharp line of her body taut. "You're throwing it all away, just like that?"

Was she putting on an act, or was this for real? It sure as fuck looked real. Same with Holt, who sat at the head of the table, bottle-feeding Lily. His expression vacillated between blank despondency and anxious fear. Either way, he hadn't liked what he'd heard; that much was real. But was it a surprise to him? Hawes's SFPD sources had reported that Chris was at the station today, but neither Holt nor Helena had been summoned for questioning. Did they know this had been in the works? Had Chris gotten the message to them? Did it matter when Hawes was certain Rose was eavesdropping from the kitchen? He had to sell this either way.

"What am I throwing away? A two-week fling with a federal agent?"

Hawes fought not to flinch at his own lie. *Fling* was too

small a word for the hurricane that had upended his world, but in the midst of the storm, he'd found something he thought out of reach for himself. Something his brother had shared with Amelia, for a time; that his parents and grandparents had been lucky to find. A steadying rod, a lover, a partner. Yes, it had only been two weeks, but Hawes knew. Chris was it for him, not just some *fling*.

"A mode of operation that's held us back."

Another lie. Hawes's rules had kept them clear of the law. Had made both their operations—legal and illegal—cleaner and easier. Less risk of life and livelihood. But that's not what Rose needed to hear.

"Let's talk about what we'd be gaining back," he argued against himself. For her benefit. "A ready-made weapons stash. Stability for the organization, inside and out. Our sister-in-law."

"The mother of my child." Holt glanced up from Lily and her bottle, his warm brown eyes both anxious and angry. "If we do this and we get caught, she could go away for even longer than what's on the table now. How does this work out for her? For me and Lily? Why not let Oak handle it? They've got Reeves on tape as the responsible party. Oak will find a way to get her off or at least reduce the charges."

It didn't work out for Amelia or for her immediate family. That realization had settled into Hawes's gut as he'd failed to fall asleep in Chris's arms last night. Amelia was just another pawn for Rose to manipulate. The only way this worked out for Amelia was to cooperate with law enforcement, which he and Chris had agreed on in the wee hours of the morning, before Chris had left the condo. But again, with Rose listening, that was the last thing Hawes could say.

"We don't have time for that. Rose needs Amelia—"

"What can Amelia offer that I can't?" Holt countered. "I'm a better hacker. Whatever Rose needs, I can do it without risking Amelia."

"You'd do that for her?" Rose entered from the kitchen, revealing herself. Tulip and Daisy trailed behind her as she rounded the table to Holt's side. "After she betrayed you?"

He aimed the same worry and ire at their grandmother, equal opportunity it seemed. And not to be cowed where his family was concerned. "She's the mother of my child."

"I need both of you."

"I can—"

"She has a part to play. She knows that." Rose squeezed Holt's shoulder. "I will protect her, I promise." Then let her hand drift lower, to run her fingers through Lily's auburn fuzz. "This is all for Lily, and I won't cause her mother, or you, any harm."

Maybe she did actually believe that, but Hawes wasn't willing to take the risk. He'd done what he could to pave an easier road for his brother's family. But even then, he wasn't taking a chance.

"And we'll have her back in custody before anyone realizes she's missing," Hawes said.

"How's that going to work?" Helena asked.

"By taking a page from your favorite movie." He retrieved two tote bags from under the table and dumped their contents out on top—brown hair dye and matching wigs. As serious as the matter was, he couldn't hold back a smile. This had been something he and Helena had talked about as kids. A heist they'd dreamed about pulling one day. He'd never thought it would be his sister-in-law they were stealing, but Hawes couldn't deny the rush that came with knowing they were actually going to do this.

Seemed Helena was feeling the same way, one side of her mouth quirking up. "We're going to *Thomas Crown* this shit?"

Hawes nodded. "She's being brought to the courthouse tomorrow morning to be arraigned on additional charges connected to the incident at MCS. We'll make the switch while she's in the Federal Building."

"We have soldiers who look close enough to make the disguises work," Rose added.

"A couple captains too," Helena said.

Hawes's stomach sank, the momentary rush skidding to a halt. If Helena was willing to bring the captains in on this, had Chris failed to get the message to her?

Motion at Helena's side, the one away from Rose, caught his attention. Five fingers spread, once, twice. *Five by five*, a saying from Helena's favorite *Buffy* character, Faith. A secret code he and Helena had picked up, which their parents and grandparents had never caught onto. She'd gotten the message, loud and clear.

Hawes's smile returned. "You going to play along?"

And Helena's grin grew wider. "We've waited our whole lives for this. Fuck yeah, I'm in."

The only one not smiling was Holt. Two steps closer and Hawes knelt beside his brother, hand on his knee.

"She's the mother of your child. We don't do this without your okay." Fuck Rose. On this, Hawes would not compromise.

"You promise to protect her?" he asked Hawes. Not Rose or Helena. That trust his twin still had in him was more of a rush than any heist they were planning to pull.

"I promise, Little H. This is all about protecting your family."

Holt's big mitt came down on top of his. "Our family."

FCI Dublin was a short walk from the ATF's Northern California division office. That was the only explanation Chris had for why Vivienne Tran was climbing into the back of the transport van where Chris waited for Amelia. He was at a complete loss, however, to explain away the signs that Tran hadn't come from the office—black jeans, gray T-shirt, leather jacket; hair loose, out of its usual bun and cascading down her back and around her face in glossy black sheets; eyes as far from flat as Chris had ever seen them. They were liquid tar, the angry heat in them dangerous, a trap for anyone who tread too close.

He scooted the opposite direction on his bench seat. "SAC Tran—"

"Save it, Perri."

The familiar bark quelled some of Chris's dissonance, but not enough that he was willing to disclose more than he had to, especially in light of Hawes's suspicion that Tran might be dirty. "Save what?" he hedged.

"The lie you're going to tell me about simply escorting Amelia Madigan to the courthouse." She slammed the doors shut behind her and claimed a spot on the bench across from him. "That's the marshals' job, not yours."

"Given the nature of the case—"

"I said save it. We don't have time."

A swerve from what had sounded like the beginning of a dressing down. So what was this, then? Even more unsure of her motives, Chris held his cards close. "Time for what?"

She shifted forward, forearms resting on her crossed knees. "Time for me to explain how this jailbreak is really going to go down."

Chris pushed back with his heels, sliding down the bench seat while drawing his gun, leveling it, two-handed, directly at his traitorous superior officer. "You're working with her?" His voice came out a rough growl, from the blistering heat of betrayal and the blistering pain in his shoulder.

Tran didn't flinch, at his voice or actions. "Yes."

"Why?"

"Because she killed my wife, and I will see her pay for that."

"Who—"

Tran twisted a finger in the bullet chain around her neck, drawing up the weight that hung below the collar of her shirt. Two rings, both coiled serpents, one studded with amethysts, the other with rubies.

Chris gasped and lowered his gun, pain temporarily sidelined by surprise. He'd seen that amethyst ring more times than he could count. On Izzy's finger. He'd never known it was a wedding band, much less that Vivienne Tran had one to match.

"Izzy was your wife?" How was that possible? Tran wasn't listed in any of Izzy's records. But given the way Tran longingly regarded the rings in her palm, Chris didn't doubt the truth staring him in the face.

"We couldn't do it officially, under the law, for too long, and then because of the agency. I was her superior, technically. We had a private commitment ceremony." She closed her eyes, and her fist around the rings, holding them to her chest. "She was my wife here, and in all the ways that counted."

While Chris's head still spun, she delivered another blow. "She'd gone dark for three days and then resurfaced only for me to be in a fucking meeting. She broke cover to leave me a voice mail. Said the mission was going to shit. I tracked her phone, but I was too late, by five fucking minutes. I got to the scene, and Hawes Madigan was on his knees beside her, where I should have been." She cast her gaze aside and swallowed hard. "Maybe if I'd gotten there in time, if I'd just answered the call, I could have saved her."

Dots connected that never had before. "That's why you covered it up. Because you wanted vengeance too."

"Vengeance... and absolution." She let the rings fall back below the collar of her shirt. "This has been the longest three years of my life, Perri. But we're so close now."

Chris reholstered his gun as he sought to connect more dots. "How did no one see you at the scene?"

"I didn't get to be SAC without some skill."

"Except Rose found out you were there," Chris speculated. There had to be some sort of leverage that connected them.

"Only because I told her," Tran said, shooting down his theory. "I went to her, told her who I was to Izzy, and told her I wanted vengeance, against Hawes."

Not leverage, a common goal. Chris peeked beneath his collar to check the bandages around his shoulder. Something mundane to counteract this wobbly reality. Except he'd gone without the sling today—he needed the extra mobility for the tasks ahead—and now his shoulder ached from the quick draw, a stark reminder of the reality of the past two weeks. Of the full weight of what Tran was saying. "You let me walk into this."

"Because that's what Izzy would have wanted. She said you were the best, and you've proven it, even if you are a giant pain in my ass. And now we have Rose right where we want her."

"Rose? Not the rest of the Madigans? You said you wanted to bring them all down. That Hawes was a target."

"For her benefit," Tran said. "She needed to think I was on her side. That the ATF was after Hawes and not her."

"So Hawes—"

"I was *there*, Perri. I saw him that night. He was on his knees, in the rain, crying as he tried to stop Izzy from bleeding out. Helena had to drag him away from the scene.

He regretted what he did, immediately. It was a terrible accident, engineered by his own grandmother."

Fucking hell, she'd known the entire time, and she'd still sent him in to infiltrate the Madigans. She couldn't have known he'd fall for Hawes, but she'd kept those details secret, from everyone. Part of him was angry at her for that omission. But another part of him understood that she couldn't disclose those details without disclosing her relationship with Izzy. Understood that those details could have compromised his cover. Understood, all too well, the lengths a person would go to to avenge the ones they loved. In any event, none of that mattered because she was right. They were so close now.

"All right," he said. "What's the plan?"

She briefly confirmed the details of the bait-and-switch plan he'd also received an encrypted message about in the wee hours of the morning.

Then Chris filled her in on his conversation with Wheeler and their suspicions about Elliot Brewster.

Tran nodded. "Rose thinks Brewster is her best bet for shoring up power. But she also hates him, even more so after the last DV charge. She's surrounded herself with powerful women, and he is a slap in the face to all that. Which is why we're going to give her an alternative."

"And now we're back to 'how this is really going to go down'..."

Tran smiled, and Chris thought maybe he'd slipped into an alternate reality. Until another blast from the past surprised him back to this one as she said, "Remy Pak."

"We have her?" Remy Pak ran guns for the Russian

mob and had been a supplier for the gang Chris had dismantled in Seattle.

"We've been on her since you hauled her in," Tran said. "She slipped up about six months ago, and she's ours now. She'll pretend to have the means to help steal back the explosives, and Rose will get the added satisfaction of double-crossing Brewster. We'll catch Rose red-handed."

"And we need Amelia to facilitate," Chris said, anticipating the play.

Tran drew two folded sheets of paper from her coat pocket. "This," she said, handing him the first, "is the signed order officially transferring Amelia into your custody, should you need it." She held out the second. "And that's the name of one of Remy's captains who was in lockup with Amelia. She just has to tell Rose that Remy reached out and wants to play ball." Tran sat back, legs crossed. "I'll drop a bug in Rose's ear too."

"What's in this for Amelia?" Chris asked as he glanced at each sheet of paper. He tucked the first into his coat pocket and kept the second out, tapping the folded crease against his knuckles. "We have to offer her something."

"Besides not extending her sentence for trying to break out of jail?"

"She was as much, if not more of a pawn than anyone," Chris countered. "She had no family before Cal brought her into the fold. Rose treated her like a grandchild, elevated her above her biological ones. And she married Holt and had the first great-grandchild. If she went against Rose, she could have lost all that."

There was a commotion outside the van. A horn blowing, voices calling for gates to open, the *clank* of metal and *whir* of gears. Amelia was on her way.

"Did she drink the Kool-Aid? Yes," Chris continued, raising his voice to be heard over the racket. "Did she have a choice? Not really."

Tran considered him a moment, dark eyes assessing, then stood. "Her cooperation won't go unnoticed."

"How much do I tell her?"

"You haven't made a wrong step yet, Agent Perri. Do what you think is best." The voices were right outside the van now. "You work your Madigan contacts, I'll work mine." Tran turned and hustled out the front of the van, disappearing from sight just as the back doors swung open.

Amelia, standing between two marshals, spotted him, and her green eyes widened. But that was the only part of her that looked alive. Despite the designer threads and heels she'd changed into for her court appearance she looked like she had aged five years in the mere five days since Chris had last seen her.

She climbed into the van, and the marshals entered behind her, long enough to attach her shackles to the hook on the floorboard and to toss Chris the key. They backed out and shut the doors behind them. A transport driver slid into the front cab, checked that they were all set, and then secured the interior doors between the cab and the back of the van, leaving Chris and Amelia alone.

When they got moving a minute later, Amelia was the first to speak. "What's going on? Anything to do with why they let me change first?"

Chris considered again his question to Tran. How

much to tell Amelia? If the past few days had taught him anything, it was that the truth got him a lot further than lies. And right now, with the way Amelia kept rubbing her right hand over her right shoulder, where he remembered she had a water lily tattoo that matched the one on Holt's chest, Chris believed that Amelia would do just about anything to get back to her daughter. She needed to trust that Chris wanted to get her there too, and that he wanted to protect her family.

Breaching the distance between them, he held out the second slip of paper Tran had given him.

Amelia took it with her chained hands. "What's this?"

"That's the key to saving yourself and your family. I'm trusting that's what you want most now." He leaned forward, making sure, even in the shadows of the van, that she could see the sincerity in his eyes. "I need you to trust that's what I want too. And that I can help you get it."

She stared down at the paper for a long moment, then green eyes lifted to meet his, and while there was a truck-load of apprehension in them, there was also a spark of hope. "How?"

Chris could work with that.

CHAPTER SEVEN

"You know you're half a foot shorter than her, right?"
A very sharp stiletto dug into the top of Hawes's foot, hard enough to sting through the brushed leather of his loafers. "That's what these five-inch Louboutins are for," Helena said. "And you're a fool if you think I'm gonna sit this one out."

He decided not to remind her that Amelia would be in similar heels, thereby obliterating her advantage. "You have a bigger role in this," he said instead. This whole plan would fall apart if she failed at either of her two critical tasks. Which was why Hawes only trusted Helena to accomplish them.

She removed her heel from his foot and buttoned her tailored suit coat. Black, same as the tailored pants and designer heels, with a simple beige top completing the outfit. All of it chosen to blend in and be easily replicated. "Don't worry, Big H. I'll take out the Klimt."

"And..." Holt prompted over the comm.

"And switch out the Renoir."

"Good, because it's showtime."

Hawes peered around Helena, out the long narrow window next to where they stood on one of the lower floors of the Federal Building. A prison van was backing up to the rear entrance, the one that led directly to the secure elevators used to transport prisoners and witnesses to the various agencies and courtrooms in the building.

"Monet on the move," Helena said, and Hawes righted his gaze in time to observe Victoria, one of their captains, striding past them toward the main bank of elevators. The doors opened to a packed cab going up, and Victoria, wearing a suit similar to Helena's, her long dark curls straightened for the occasion, slid inside.

"Cézanne on fifteen," Alice radioed. "Inside Judge Riley's chambers." Which were located directly across from the witness and prisoner holding rooms used for the federal courtrooms on the same floor.

Alice, the blonde captain with a passing resemblance to Helena, was likewise pulling double duty, first posing as Helena to get into the secure area, then donning a wig for her next role, to come shortly.

The real Helena hip-checked Hawes. "The artists are a nice touch."

"It was your idea." Decades ago, before they knew their prize or the very real complications involved in this heist. But it was the least he could do to show his appreciation for his sister, who always had his back, especially in this, their future.

She rose on tiptoes and kissed his cheek. "Thank you

for remembering." And then she was gone, skirting past him toward the stairs. "Van Gogh on the move."

"Don't lose an ear," Hawes added, and chuckled at the middle finger she shot him as she disappeared into the stairwell.

"Eyes on Renoir and da Vinci," Holt reported, and Hawes snapped his gaze back to the window, to the man and woman exiting the van outside. Mostly to the man. Had it only been thirty hours since he'd lain in those arms? It felt like a lifetime. And with no idea when he might get the chance again, a lifetime felt like fucking eternity. But they couldn't risk it, not until this was over, which meant this heist had to go off without a hitch. They needed to move on to whatever Rose planned next so they could set the final trap for her. So they could be done with this and Hawes could get back to the life, to the future, he'd just begun to think possible.

As the van pulled away, a Madigan soldier, Eva, dressed in the same black suit, with her normally dyed bright hair now a sedate brown, appeared and passed close by Chris. Their hands brushed, too passing a touch for a casual observer to notice. "Munch has made the handoff," Hawes said.

Eva continued on to the sidewalk, while Chris and Amelia made their way to the entry doors, Chris rubbing at his right ear. A moment later there was a *click*, and Holt confirmed, "Da Vinci is live."

Chris grumbled, "Very funny," and Hawes had to stifle a laugh with his hand.

"Well, we couldn't use Dan—" Helena sniped, only to

be cut off by Holt. "Da Vinci and Renoir are in the elevator."

"Rembrandt on the move," Hawes said, forestalling any further verbal sparring. He'd spotted his mark—one of the federal judges' clerks. The chambers access badge Hawes needed hung from the pocket of the hipster's corduroy jacket, right where Helena said it would be. He followed the clerk into the crowded elevator, and ninety seconds and a little pickpocketing later, exited onto the fifteenth floor, the rectangular piece of plastic in his palm. "Access secured."

"Monet, Gauguin," Holt said. "You're up."

With federal courtrooms on either side of the expansive lobby, jurors, attorneys, press, and even a tour group filled the high-traffic area. And among them, half a dozen brunettes in the same dark suit, slipping in and out of courtrooms, like any other legal or court personnel. Hawes had to concentrate to track each one, to catch the do-si-do two of their operatives, Gayle and Sue, executed, before they headed in opposite directions. It was masterful, and Hawes regretted Helena wasn't here to see all the moving parts in action, including Victoria and Elisabeth—Monet and Gauguin—break out into an argument in the middle of the lobby. As intended, the escalating altercation drew the armed guard off the door marked Authorized Personnel Only.

Hawes approached the door—not too fast, not too slow —not wanting to redraw the guard's attention and giving Holt time to blind the eye in the sky, the black bubble cam right over the door.

"Countdown for Rembrandt," Holt said, and Hawes took a step closer with each tick. "Three. Two. One. Clear."

Hawes flashed the access card, the lock turned green, and he pushed through like he had every right to do so. Again, less likely to draw attention. The door had barely shut behind him when a deep, surprised voice sounded over a comm. "Amelia, what—"

Oakland Ashe's words died, a *thump* followed, then silence. They had ten seconds, at most, before their timing was shot. It only took five. "Klimt is down," Helena confirmed.

"Excuse me, sir."

Hawes's gaze shot up, meeting that of the bailiff at the end of the hallway closest to the stairs.

"You're not supposed to be back here," the older man said.

Behind the bailiff, the stairwell door banged open and Helena emerged, looking more like herself with the dark wig gone. "Sorry, Jimmy," she said, laying a hand on the big man's arm. "Hawes knows the rules but getting him to follow them is a full-time job."

Hawes reached into his coat, dropped the access card into his pocket, and withdrew a photo of Lily. "Just wanted to give this"—he stepped closer and held up the picture —"to my sister-in-law. It's her daughter."

The drawn *V* of the bailiff's brows eased as he looked from Helena to the photo to Hawes, then deepened again when he looked past Hawes to the lobby door. "How did you—" And then deeper still as his gaze skittered farther down the hall to the opening elevator doors. "You're not the usual marshal."

Chris held up his badge one-handed, his other hand over Amelia's cuffed wrists at her back, as they stepped into the hallway. "Special Agent Christopher Perri. ATF. Relieved the marshal as she's our prisoner. I have the paperwork, if you need it."

Amelia looked like hell. Pale skin, limp hair, dark circles under her dull green eyes. Hawes worried maybe this wouldn't work, the surface appearances not close enough, but the way Amelia still carried herself—proud and alert, shoulders back, chin held high, and eyes darting around the hallway—would be the things a stranger recognized first. Those mannerisms were replicable, and the rest was close enough. Assuming Amelia, who was clearly assessing escape routes, didn't make a break for it and fuck this whole operation. And assuming Chris had been able to convince her to help them, not Rose.

Either way, they were out of time, Holt giving the next order. "Monet, Cézanne, go."

Between where Hawes stood and where Chris and Amelia had halted, Alice, dark wig on now, appeared out of Judge Riley's chambers, and across from her, the lobby door opened again, admitting Elisabeth. The operatives bumbled into each other mid-hallway, a few feet from Chris and Amelia, and with the three women similarly styled, and Chris also in black jeans, a black leather coat, and his long dark hair loose, it was a virtual traffic jam of sameness. If the bailiff's face were an emoji just then, it would have been the head-exploding one.

Helena pounced, stepping closer to him. "So, Jimmy, about that offer you made on the Ducati. I might be willing to consider it." Suddenly, she had all the big man's attention.

And in that instant, in a blink, Amelia's freed hands dropped to her sides, she spun one way, Elisabeth the other, and in the next blink, Elisabeth was beside Chris in Amelia's place, hands behind her back.

And Amelia was free. Her eyes cut to the lobby door, and it took everything in Hawes not to step her direction, to trust that Chris had come through and that Amelia would put her daughter first.

His trust was not unfounded.

Alice struck up a conversation with Amelia as if they were besties, and Amelia played along, looping an arm through Alice's, and together, they exited back out to the lobby. The door shut behind them, and Alice reported through the comms, "Renoir secured."

Helena didn't miss a beat, shifting the bailiff's attention back to the people in the hallway so he wouldn't dwell on the two who'd just left it. "Seriously, Hawes, you have to go."

Chris stepped around him and handed Elisabeth over to the bailiff. "Transferring her into your custody."

Jimmy did a double take, eyes narrowing. Before the bailiff's suspicions could take form, Hawes handed Elisabeth the picture of Lily and leaned in to kiss her cheek. "Holt wanted you to have this. They miss you."

Elisabeth's eyes filled with tears, and she lowered her chin, hair falling forward and obscuring her face.

Preventing further examination. Hawes made a mental note to elevate her to lieutenant.

"Shall we?" Helena said, gesturing toward the courtroom.

"You're representing her now?" Jimmy asked. "I thought Oak—"

"Had a family emergency. Just filling in." She handed him a sheet of paper. "Temporary substitution of counsel." It had been a stipulation of the retainer when they'd hired Oak to represent Amelia. If for some reason Oak couldn't make a court date, or was removed from the case, Helena would be able to step right in. An emergency measure. This wasn't the emergency any of them had had in mind, but it was an advantage they were willing to use under the circumstances.

"I'll need to clear this with the clerk," Jimmy said.

"Of course," Helena said. "We can finish discussing the Ducati while we wait. Inside?"

Interest piqued again, Jimmy moved for the door, then paused, glancing back at Hawes. Chris was already at his side, hand on his arm in an official-like capacity. "I actually need to question this one in our offices." Just a couple of floors away in the building.

Jimmy bought it. "Thank you, Agent."

They walked to the stairwell door, slow enough to be sure Jimmy admitted Helena and Elisabeth into the courtroom, and slow enough for Holt to confirm the stairwell cameras were still under his control. Once inside, Hawes slumped against the wall and exhaled. The next instant, a warm body crowded his, surrounded him, and he inhaled eucalyptus, leather, and coffee, and tasted the man he'd been craving.

Tongues and teeth clashed, and Chris slid his hands down Hawes's arms, caught his wrists, and hauled them up above his head. Pinning him to the wall, their bodies stretched and aligned, almost as close as they could be. Hawes grunted his agreement and hitched a leg around Chris's, closing that last bit of distance, bringing them hard dick to hard dick, and thrusting. Letting go and letting Chris hold him up, burn him up. Fuck, he needed...

"You two cannot fuck in a public stairwell," Holt grumbled over the comm.

Hawes tore his mouth from Chris's long enough to bark, "Stop fucking creeping."

Chris shook with laughter, his brown eyes alight with desire and humor. "As much as I want to fuck you right now, he's right. And if I keep my left arm up here like this, I won't be able to help you move that tree."

"Plus, bogeys five flights away," Holt said. "So cut the make-out session short and move it."

Chris trailed his hands down Hawes's arms, making him shiver, then stepped away. Hawes pouted as he peeled himself off the wall. "Do we have the Renoir?"

"Renoir clear," Alice said. "On our way to the mountain."

"Copy that." Hawes removed the comm from his ear and motioned for Chris to do the same. "Do we really have her?" he asked Chris.

"I hope so."

Not the answer he wanted. "Hope isn't good—"

Chris curled a hand around Hawes's neck, thumb coaxing Hawes's tightening jaw to relax again. "I'm trusting so."

Better answer, and Chris's confidence went a long way to reassuring him.

"Do you trust me?" Chris said.

Hawes kissed him in answer, stealing one more taste, before reluctantly returning to the task at hand. "Let's go move a tree."

CHAPTER EIGHT

Hawes navigated the SUV up Fassler, routinely checking his rearview mirror for tails. None that he could discern. Only a few cars straggled around him on the winding road up from the Pacific Coast Highway and into Pacifica's canyons. He reached up and angled the mirror down, checking on the VIP immediately behind him. Thumb in her mouth, Lily remained fast asleep. She'd been fussy the last time they'd brought her out here, the twists and turns tough on her tummy and the climbing altitude no kinder on her ears. But all the activity this morning —a surprise trip to Uncle Brax's place, then a few hours at MCS—must have tuckered her out.

"She's good," Holt said from the passenger seat beside him.

"What did you tell Brax when you picked her up?"

Holt continued to tap and swipe at his tablet. "Same as I told him when I dropped her off. That the three of us were needed in court and that her godfather was the only other person I trusted to keep her safe."

"Maybe we should have left—"

"I'm not keeping her from Amelia."

"It's not Amelia I'm worried about." Granted, Hawes's sister-in-law could still change her mind—God only knew what Rose had told her in the hours since she'd escaped custody—but given how shaken Amelia had looked under her put-on poise, and how confident Chris had been in her cooperation, Hawes considered her more likely than not to side with them. And he had zero concerns about Lily's safety during this visit. Amelia just wanted to hold her daughter again; that much was obvious, the signs of separation anxiety written all over her face.

No, the one Hawes was worried about was Rose, who would no doubt ask why they were keeping Lily from *her*. What more would she ask of them? Another scheme that risked their lives and freedom? A job that required them to leave Lily with her while they did her dirty work? Hawes clutched the steering wheel, knuckles white, as he summoned his control and steeled himself for the conversation ahead.

"The name Chris gave you checks out," Holt said. "She's a captain for Remy Pak and was Amelia's cellmate, for a night. I doubt they talked much, but Rose won't know that."

"And Pak?" Hawes had heard of the Russian mob lieutenant, but she was relatively new in San Francisco's criminal circles.

"Her bosses brought her in to try and get a bigger piece in the weapons trade here. She's got reach."

Holt held up his tablet, screen toward Hawes, so he could take a quick peek. Hawes whistled low. On-screen, red dots were scattered up and down a map of the West Coast.

"That's everywhere her name is mentioned on the dark web in connection with *explosives* and similar words."

"Does the ATF really have her?" Hawes asked.

"She was hauled into the Seattle field office about a year ago."

"When Chris was there?"

Holt nodded. "She was tangled up with the gang he busted up there. Suspected of dealing AKs and other weapons to them."

"So this will also look like vengeance against him." Or maybe it was actual payback too. With a wildcard like Pak, Hawes couldn't discount the possibility, regardless of any cooperation she promised the ATF. "Business adjustments since the bust?" Hawes asked, from his own experience.

"Not then," Holt answered. "Six months ago, though, she set up a trust fund for someone named Samantha Smith. Next day, Pak left San Diego, where she'd been since leaving Seattle."

"Samantha Smith. Relatively generic." Though something about the name tickled the back of Hawes's mind. Something familiar.

"Alias?"

"Likely," Holt replied, then lapsed into silence. The quiet, however, only lasted a few minutes, long enough for them to crest the hill into Park Pacifica and turn onto Grand Teton, their destination imminent. "If Perri and his boss are wrong," Holt said, "we could be giving Rose exactly what she wants. A dangerous new ally."

"I trust him." Hawes thought back to their too brief respite in the Federal Building stairwell, to the trust that had flowed between them, to the steadiness it had provided in a sea of swirling chaos. "I know it doesn't make any sense—I've only known him for two weeks, and he's a fucking fed—but the way you trust Brax, that's how much I trust Chris."

Surprising Hawes, Holt let out a short, sharp laugh. "I trusted Brax the second I stepped off that army transport in the desert, and I had no idea who he even was. He was just some captain in a uniform at the bottom of the plane's stairs, but when he lifted his shades and introduced himself as our unit leader, I knew I was going to be okay. So I get it." He tossed his tablet onto the dash and angled toward Hawes. "But it's not Perri I'm worried about," he said, repeating Hawes's earlier words.

And the sentiment applied the same, though in this case, it wasn't only Rose. Tactically, they also had to worry about Pak, Tran, Brewster, and their soldiers, whose allegiance was still unknown for the most part. There were multiple wildcards, and yet only one viable play on the board. "It's the best option we've got," Hawes said. "But the tip has to come from Amelia. Rose won't buy it otherwise."

"I'll talk to Amelia, if she doesn't come through."

Hawes slowed to a stop in front of the fixer-upper Holt

had purchased earlier that year, and put the SUV in park, turning the wheels toward the curb. He unbuckled his seat belt and shifted to face his twin. "Are you ready for this?"

Holt's gaze drifted out the window toward the house. "I thought we'd fix this place up and it would be our home. Something Amelia and I could call our own. A nice place in a nice neighborhood to raise a family. And now..."

The dejection in his broken voice and the slump of his giant shoulders made every part of Hawes hurt. Made him grieve for his brother and for the happily ever after that Hawes himself had aspired to. "Holt..."

"She befriended me at a time when all I wanted to do was push people away, and she made me laugh. It was only the second time I'd been attracted to someone, the only time I'd fallen in love, and she didn't think that was weird. She took me to the shelter, introduced me to a demi friend of hers, and for the first time since I'd come home, I didn't feel alone. I didn't feel invisible. But now I don't know how much of that to believe. Was she actually attracted to me— did she love me—or was she just following our grandparents' orders? Was she just humoring me and my sexuality?" With every question, Holt's voice grew louder, more strained, fear, despair, and anger riding him hard. Hawes wanted to reach out and comfort him, but before he could get in a word, Holt was speaking again, the rising anger reddening his cheeks under his beard. "And while she was bettering my life, for real or not, she was ruining Max Bailey's, convincing him to drive that van that almost killed you. I was his sponsor! How can I ever trust her again? She lied to me for years." His last word was barely a whisper, fury having run its course and despair taking over. Holt dropped his gaze to his lap, where he clasped his shaking hands. "I'm scared," he rasped out. "I'm scared I won't find that connection again, with her or anyone."

Hawes covered his brother's hands with one of his. "Don't count Amelia out. Chris wasn't who he said he was at first either."

"But he was, Hawes. Underneath it all, Perri was who he said he was. I don't know who Amelia is, other than the mother of my child."

Hawes squeezed his hands, then unbuckled his brother's seat belt. "Then you focus on that."

"But what she did the week before last—" Holt's words cut off as he got tangled in the seat-belt strap, the man too big for his own good. Freeing himself, eventually, he let the strap fly with a huff, and the buckle clanked against the window.

Hawes couldn't help but laugh, and after a moment, so did Holt, the tension in the vehicle eased by the unexpected, mundane battle. Behind them, Lily snuffled as she began to wake. Hawes retrieved the tablet off the dash and handed it to Holt. "Focus on what Amelia did today and how she helped us last week."

They unloaded from the car, Hawes bringing Lily in her carrier around to Holt and trading off for the diaper bag. They walked up the cracked cement path to the front porch, and Hawes opened the door, ushering Holt and Lily inside. Holt stalled in the foyer, and Hawes nearly ran into his back. Glancing around Holt's shoulder, he spotted Amelia at the top of the split-level stairs. The smile that graced her face, the happiness that lit her eyes, was all Hawes needed to see. They'd made the right call trusting her, and Chris.

From the lower level, someone cleared their throat, demanding his attention. Helena waited at the bottom of the stairs, her barely contained fury the polar opposite of Amelia's joy. She mouthed, *"Get down here,"* and Hawes hustled to comply.

Hanging the diaper bag over Holt's shoulder, Hawes nudged his brother up the stairs and cringed as they groaned under his weight. The entire house needed structural reinforcement, the decks on both levels needed to be totally rebuilt, and as Hawes descended the rickety stairs into the very unfinished lower level, he thought, for the umpteenth time, about telling Holt—*again*—to just tear it all down and start over. Busted ductwork and insulation hung from the open ceiling, the Sheetrock on the walls was intermittent, errant wires hung low, and the slab floor dipped and rose under Hawes's feet. The only light in the dank space came from the two windows in the far wall and from the standing lamp in the adjacent room, visible through the gaps in the Sheetrock. Rose sat in the halo of its golden glow, a single folder on the table in front of her.

Helena fell into step beside him, and they moved toward the room where Rose waited. Unfortunately, all the open walls made it impossible to ask what fresh hell Rose had planned for them next. "Any complications?" he asked his sister instead.

"None," she said, then under her breath, "Until five minutes ago," before leading him into the room with Rose.

"Elisabeth is in local lockup until tomorrow afternoon. The ATF helpfully indicated they may need to question her further. We'll have to make the switch back before the transport leaves for FCI Dublin at three."

"Phase two, then?" Hawes said to Rose. "We freed Amelia as you requested, but time is tight."

"I have another job for you first." She pushed the folder across the table toward them. "Nicholas Ferriello's birthday party is tonight at Club Sterling. In attendance will also be Antonin Volz and Patrick McKennie."

"Three of our active targets." Helena tried not to seethe and failed. Whether because of Rose or the targets, Hawes couldn't say. This obvious test when they were on the clock was ridiculous. And the three targets were targets for a reason. A ruthless merc whose playboy ways got people killed, a prickly German arms dealer with zero scruples about whom he traded with, and the Irish mob's racist blowhard and hit man of choice.

"You didn't have any problem taking out targets at that auction you engineered last week," Rose said. "You wanted to make a show of power then. I want to make one now, for our *entire* family."

In a popular nightclub, full of innocents. This was dangerous; the potential for collateral damage was enormous. None of that mattered to Rose. But why didn't the more effective show of power—stealing back the explosives—matter more?

"Why are we really doing this?" he asked.

"We have an opportunity," Rose said. "A potential new

ally, but given the recent upheaval in our organization, she requires a demonstration."

"And you want to test us." Helena didn't hide the affront in her voice. "Again."

"Can you blame me?" Rose countered. "None of you even trust me with my great-granddaughter. You don't trust me, and yet you expect me to trust you again with this organization."

Hawes shared his sister's indignation, and his concern for Lily was at the forefront of his mind once more. But also there, with the anger and anxiety, was a burgeoning sense of victory that had Hawes clutching his hands behind his back, controlling the urge to fist-pump. He had a good idea where this was headed, and it was the direction he wanted. "How did this new ally come to us?" he asked Rose, seeking to confirm his suspicion.

"I can answer that," Amelia said, appearing over the threshold with Lily in her arms. "One of her captains was my cellmate at Dublin."

"Who did your cellmate work for?" Hawes asked.

"Remy Pak."

Hawes nearly crushed his fingers to keep from smiling.

Hawes secured Lily's carrier in the car seat base and tucked her diaper bag on the floor. When he straightened and turned, he found himself caged in, Helena standing at the open door.

"What am I missing?" she demanded.

"Keep it down." He ducked under her arm and circled to the rear of the SUV, an incensed Helena on his heels. Resting against the bumper, he positioned himself and Helena so that he could keep an eye on the house while also preventing Rose from having too close an eye on their conversation. "Remy Pak is in the ATF's pocket."

To her credit, Helena schooled her features, not expressing the surprise that colored her voice. "You sure about that?"

"Can we ever be sure with people in our business?"

"Accurate." Helena began tapping her nails, and Hawes discreetly knocked her hand. He needed this convo to appear casual, not nerve-racking. She cursed, and Hawes thought it was directed at him, until she crossed her arms so her hands were tucked. "At least she's a better option than that asshole Brewster."

"That's why Chris's boss put Pak in Rose's path."

Face angled toward him, she arched a brow. "I thought this came through Amelia?"

"Through her, yes, but planted by Tran, whom Rose called to confirm that Amelia and Pak's captain had in fact shared a cell."

"Chris's boss is Rose's mole at the ATF?"

"Not exactly." Hawes laid a hand on her biceps, ready to stop her if surprise sent her flying off the bumper. "Tran was Isabella's wife."

Beneath Hawes's hand, Helena strained to hold still as she muttered a, "Holy fuck."

"Accurate," Hawes parroted back.

Helena lifted a hand, started to run it down her face,

then corrected, lifting the other and pulling her hair into a ponytail with the elastic around her right wrist. "This op has disaster written all over it. Putting aside trying to figure out who is playing who, the potential for collateral damage at Sterling is massive."

That had been his first thought too, until he'd considered the upsides. How they could roll this morning's victory into an even bigger one. How they could swing the momentum their direction. "Yes, it's risky, but we can use it to our advantage."

Helena side-eyed him. "You've got that look. The same one you had when you thought flying solo at that auction was a good idea."

"It worked out in the end." To their advantage professionally and to his personally, resulting in a fight that led to a breakthrough—and blowjob—with Chris. Hawes could make this job work out for them too, professionally at least. Handling the personal aspect with Chris would be tricky—he would no doubt protest that it was too risky—but Helena was the person Hawes had to convince first. "Rose won't be at the club. We'll be out from under her nose. Let's use this op to take care of some other business. To shore up our forces."

"You want to meet with the captains."

Hawes nodded. "Those involved this morning were spectacular. They deserve to hear that, from both of us, and they need to know what our plan is going forward. Most importantly, they're the only operatives I trust to minimize collateral damage at the club."

"While also showing Rose what she needs to see."

"Exactly."

"Speaking of..." She flicked her gaze toward the house, and Hawes shifted for a better view. Rose, Holt, and Amelia, with Lily in her arms, had emerged onto the porch. The tension between Amelia and Holt was apparent, but so was the fact that they were standing together... and apart from Rose.

A good sign.

"I'll get the captains ready," Helena said, then pushed off the bumper and strode toward the sedan where Holt was leading Rose. Amelia carried Lily to the SUV, and Hawes opened the rear door on the side with the car seat.

"Thank you," Hawes said, "for helping us."

"I'm helping my daughter." Amelia buckled Lily into the seat. "And Perri said my cooperation would be repaid."

"If he doesn't make it happen, I will."

She kissed Lily's head, then righted herself, turning sharp green eyes on Hawes. Assessing him, like she'd done in that court hallway this morning. Thankfully, she came to the same conclusion. "Thank you," she returned as she softly, reluctantly closed the car door.

"You'll be okay here?" Hawes asked.

"Are you asking if I'll run?"

"No, I'm asking if you'll be okay here. It's not exactly a livable structure yet."

"It's got power. I'll manage. And I have work to do."

Hawes caught her by the elbow before she started back toward the house. They hadn't had a moment alone together until now—he didn't know when they might have another—and there was another dangling thread on his mind. "We found and decrypted your backup. It didn't contain any information on Isabella."

"Who's your priority, Hawes? Perri or your family?"

Same thing, or as near as, with respect to his future, but that wasn't the answer Amelia wanted to hear. She wanted the answer that best protected her daughter. "My priority is putting all of this to bed so our family can move forward, and as far as I can tell, the situation escalated to the point of no return the night Isabella died."

"You uphold your end of this bargain, and I'll cooperate, fully."

Meaning she had more to tell. The whole truth was still out there, and Hawes would do whatever it took to get it, for Chris and for all of them.

CHAPTER NINE

Two hard raps on the front door drew Chris's attention from the Club Sterling blueprints spread on his kitchen island.

"You expecting company?" Tran asked from across the island. "Madigans?"

Chris checked his personal cell first. No texts from his family. He flipped over the encrypted burner. No messages from any of the Madigans either, not that they ever bothered to knock when showing up unannounced. "No idea."

More hard knocks echoed down the hallway.

"Whoever it is," Tran said, "get rid of them. We're on the clock."

She wasn't wrong. T-minus two hours until showtime.

Adjusting the sling he'd put back on, Chris strode down the long narrow hall and opened the door to Braxton Kane. Eyes hard, face drawn, the chief looked stressed out and pissed off. He didn't wait for Chris to invite him in. He pushed inside and rounded on Chris as soon as the door closed behind them. "What the fuck is going on?"

"Plausible—"

Chris's words died as his back hit the wall, Kane's forearm shoved under his chin. "Fuck plausible deniability. This is my family."

"How's that, Chief Kane?" Tran asked.

Kane's gaze whipped to the side, and his hazel eyes widened, round as dinner plates. Chris had probably looked much the same that morning when he'd first glimpsed this stripped-down version of Vivienne Tran.

"Your last name's not Madigan," she said. "You're no blood relation. Leave, while you still can."

Chris was fairly certain Kane couldn't leave at this point either, but he offered him the out anyway. "Still want to fuck plausible deniability?" he croaked out around Kane's forearm.

Kane stepped back, but he didn't turn for the door. He lifted his chin and gritted out, "Yes."

As Chris expected. Kane was too invested, same as Chris. Readjusting the sling, Chris followed the chief into the kitchen.

"What are these?" Kane asked, eyeing the floor plans on the island.

"Blueprints for Club Sterling," Tran said.

"Where a Madigan op is going down tonight," Chris added.

"The explosives?" Kane asked. "Surely they aren't there. Rose isn't that reckless."

"It's another test," Chris said, and proceeded to fill

Kane in on the details Hawes had shared with him that afternoon. "And an audition for a potential new ally."

"Who?"

Tran gave a single shake of her head, sharp enough that glossy black strands escaped her ponytail.

Chris ignored her. He wasn't changing his approach now, especially not with one of the few people involved in this mess whom he trusted completely. "Remy Pak."

Fuming, Tran yanked the elastic out of her hair, the rest of it falling free, as she stalked away from them, toward the back of the condo, muttering "insubordinate fucker" curses and "fire his ass" promises.

"Pak runs weapons for the Russian mob," Kane said, continuing to track Tran with his gaze. "She hit our radar when she flew into SFO. I do not want her in my fucking city, and she is not a player we want in Rose's corner."

"She's working with the ATF," Chris said, and Kane's gaze snapped back to him.

"So this is an ATF op tonight? Why wasn't SFPD notified?"

"Because," Tran said, pacing back their direction, "SFPD will not be involved tonight. And neither will the ATF, except to observe."

"We're going to let this play out," Chris explained.

Kane shoved the blueprints aside and planted a hand on the tiles, facing Chris directly. If he'd been pissed off before, he was fucking furious now. "Remember what I told you a while back? I do not want a bloodbath in my city, and I do not want my family dead in its streets."

Tran came at them like a tornado, shoving Chris aside

and getting right in Kane's face. "My family did die in these streets, and you"—she jabbed Kane's chest with an accusatory finger—"helped cover it up."

Gasping, Kane wobbled back a step, and Chris shifted to avoid a collision. He'd had that fire directed at him before—Tran having chewed him out on the regular—but never had it been so scalding or so personal. It made him doubt the trust he'd put in her. While he understood Rose was the architect of Izzy's death, he wasn't sure Tran wouldn't shoot Hawes given the chance.

"Fuck," Kane muttered, recovering his voice. "Isabella?"

"They were married," Chris replied when Tran didn't; then, as another wife came to mind, his gaze slid sideways, avoiding Kane's.

The top cop caught the dodge. "What else aren't you telling me?"

Chris took another step back, out of reach of any punch Kane might throw. "Amelia's back in play."

If Chris had thought the chief's eyes dinner-plate wide before, they were the size of turkey platters now. "She's not in custody?"

"Do you really want me to answer that question?"

"This morning, Holt dropped off Lily..."

Chris didn't nod or shake his head.

Kane figured out the answer easily enough. He turned away, his motions stilted as he skimmed a hand over his head. "For once, I'd just like to not be the last person to know everything."

"They're protecting you, Brax."

"But I'm the cop." He sounded weary, as close to broken as Chris had ever heard him. "I'm the one who swore to protect and serve. I've protected him...them..."

Chris laid a hand on his forearm, noticing for the first time the intricate tattoos there. They were usually covered by his shirt sleeves, which now that Chris thought about it, were never rolled up. He shook away the momentary distraction. "Let them protect you for a change."

"It's your day off, Chief Kane," Tran said, resuming her position on the other side of the island. "Go home and forget this conversation ever happened."

Kane's defeated daze only broke when they reached the front door. "Should I expect babysitting duty tonight?" he asked, one foot over the threshold.

"No, Rose will keep an eye on her." The words sounded as wrong to Chris as they must have felt to Kane, who lurched forward and grasped either side of the doorframe.

"Why the fuck would they do that?"

"She was suspicious about why they were keeping Lily from her. Why Holt brought her to you this morning instead."

"But what if she—"

What if she kidnapped Holt's daughter, Kane's goddaughter? It was the same fear that had gripped Chris when he'd woken up in that hospital bed on Saturday. The worry was no less acute now, and the risk was even greater. Which was why Kane couldn't be at the club tonight. He had someplace more important to be— on a stakeout to protect their most vulnerable family member. "I think you know where you need to be tonight."

"Fuck." He pushed off the doorframe and stalked a frustrated circle on the porch, before turning back to Chris. "I'll stake out the house, call if she moves. I'm counting on *you* to keep the rest of them safe."

For a split second, Chris felt as weary as Kane looked, but then Chris remembered Hawes in this condo last week —how he'd made it feel like home again for the first time in years—and answered without any further hesitation. "Trust me."

Helena closed the door behind Victoria, muting the thumping bass of the club music downstairs. Normally, Hawes didn't mind the deafening racket of a packed club. He loved dancing, loved getting lost in the music and the sea of swaying bodies. Aside from sex, it was one of the only other times he let his control slip. But he couldn't let anything slip tonight. So he let the rumbling vibration of the music steady him instead, imagined the rhythmic beat was that of the heart of the man on the other end of the burner phone in his pocket. There if Hawes needed him, always keeping him steady.

He perched next to Helena on the edge of the manager's desk and eyed the captains spread around the room. Despite their seemingly relaxed positions—Alice and Malik on the chaise, Austin and Grant on top of a low filing cabinet, Gayle, Sue, and Connor at the round table in the corner, and Victoria on the arm of the chair where the lone lieutenant, Avery, sat—all of them were alert and ready for the op. And all of them but Avery regarded him cautiously, their eyes frequently darting to Helena for their cues. Which was why Hawes, after commending the captains involved in that morning's operation and elevating Victoria and Alice, and the absent Elisabeth, to lieutenants, turned the floor over to his sister.

A ripple of surprise swept the room, cresting before the wave crashed into Helena. Her confused blue eyes landed on him, and Hawes hoped she saw in their reflection all the confidence he had in her. The people in this room trusted him only so far, but they trusted Helena implicitly. That was the loyalty they needed tonight. He would prove himself through his actions; his sister already had. They needed to hear the plan—the orders—from her. "You're the impressive one."

She cast her gaze aside and inhaled deeply. Hopefully, as he'd intended, she was recalling the conversation they'd had after Papa Cal's death. That day in the garden, she'd called Holt the brave one, him the strong one, and herself the scared one. All true, except all three of them were scared, unsure of what the future would hold and scared for their loved ones. But despite that fear, she'd held it together and held their coalition together too.

Impressive.

He scooted closer, enough to give her a subtle hip check and draw her gaze back to him. Love, loyalty, and appreciation shined in her eyes, and he would have wrapped her in a crushing hug if not for their present circumstances. A smile would have to do, and he didn't bother hiding how wide or full of pride it was. He wanted the captains and lieutenants to see that too.

She returned the grin, then straightened and stepped forward, shoulders back and arms loose at her sides. Confident, like she could spring and kill at any second. "You have a choice to make tonight: the past or the future." She addressed the team like she addressed a jury, the lawyer in her coming out as she made her opening statement. "You're all aware of the recent tension in the organization."

"Because he slept with a fed," Connor said.

"No," Helena said. "Because our grandmother had a fed killed."

"He pulled the trigger," Victoria said.

Hawes internally winced at the mention of that night —the mental film reel of it impossible to pause—but the identity of the speaker did not give him pause. He respected Victoria even more for voicing it, despite the promotion he'd just bestowed on her. He wanted independent thinkers, not blind followers.

"I did," Hawes said. "And I've tried to do better every day since."

"I've seen it," Helena said. "You've all seen it. No indiscriminate killing. No collateral damage. No unvetted targets. Hawes's rules have kept us safe. Kept us as clean as we can be in this business."

"So why does Rose want to get rid of them?" Alice asked.

"Power. Profit she thinks we're leaving on the table. A notion that the old ways are better."

"Sometimes they are," Connor replied, and the twitch of Helena's hand reflected the niggle of worry swirling in Hawes's gut. Connor was their most junior captain, promoted earlier that year. Had Rose and Amelia recruited him while he was still a soldier?

In any event, Malik shut him down. "Usually they aren't."

"Our city, our world, is changing," Helena said, taking back the reins of the conversation. "We have to change with it. That's what my brothers and I are trying to do."

Hawes braced as Connor opened his mouth to speak again. "Why were we sidelined?" the captain asked, and Hawes better understood the young man's simmering resentment. Was relieved by it, as it was something they could work with, to their benefit.

Helena was on it already. "That was Rose and Amelia's decision," she told Connor. "They manipulated the other lieutenants and soldiers."

"And left me out," Avery said, "so I know how you feel."

Hawes recalled the chart on Chris's wall, thought about where Rose and Amelia had struck within their organization—at connections that were either long established, meaning the lieutenants, or not established enough, meaning the soldiers. "They left you out, Avery," he said, "because you were the most recent captain promoted. They left all of you out because you were not as easily influenced as soldiers nor as tied in as longtime lieutenants. You are the independents."

"And you outnumber us, up and down," Helena said.

"This is as much, if not more your organization than ours. You make this call."

"What are we being asked to do?" Victoria inquired.

"Our grandmother's ultimate goal is to steal back the explosives seized by the ATF. Then she wants to sell them to the highest bidder, which is currently Elliot Brewster."

Curses and scoffs bounced off the walls, and disgusted faces were had by all. Hawes's earlier pride in his sister expanded to each of their colleagues in this room. They'd picked their people well, and Rose and Amelia had done them the favor of weeding out the bad apples.

"That's the past," Helena said.

"And the future?" Alice prompted.

"Wants nothing to do with explosives. We don't need them. We're assassins. Explosives look powerful, but they aren't the source of our power. They aren't our primary skill." Helena reached behind her, lifted her leather jacket, and withdrew her Sig. "We don't need these either." She set the gun on the coffee table in front of the chaise.

Pride and affection swelled for his sister, but Hawes worried it was too much of an ask, given the sudden quiet among the others. "Hena, you don't have to—"

Helena, however, pushed on. "There's another potential bidder. One we prefer, though it is not our intention to actually go through with the heist and sale." She didn't go so far as to name Remy, or to indicate she was an ATF plant, or that they were working with the ATF, but she didn't need to to make their point to this audience. "The new bidder requires a demonstration, as does Rose. But I want to do it on our terms. On the path we"—she gestured at herself and Hawes—"want to take into the future. The question is, are you with us?"

Malik didn't hesitate. He rose from the chaise and set his gun beside Helena's. "The past is rarely ever the right way to go."

Avery was fast on his heels, her loyalty already proven. Victoria and Alice were a tad slower to follow, but once they'd made their allegiance known, the rest of the captains fell in line. Everyone except Connor, who instead came to stand in front of Hawes and Helena.

"I trust you," he said to Helena, handing her his gun. His dark eyes shifted to Hawes. "I'm not sure how much I trust you."

Hawes surprised him by clasping his shoulder. "I have to earn back your trust, that's fair. But your trust in Helena is enough for now."

CHAPTER TEN

I t had been years since Chris had stepped foot inside the building that now housed Club Sterling. Back then, it had been some generic seafood place. From what Chris recalled, the drinks and views had been better than the actual food. Situated on the Embarcadero, in the shadow of the Bay Bridge, the cavernous space boasted floor-to-ceiling windows that provided unparalleled vistas of the Bay and the bridge.

Now, as a high-end nightclub for San Francisco's rich and powerful, legal and otherwise, the location, space, and sleek, modern decor were likewise unparalleled—from the polished-wood bar at one end, to the dance floor that stretched out in front of it, to the brick wall at the far end where a steel staircase led to the mezzanine. Under the mezzanine overhang, polished steel and leather booths provided main floor seating and more gleaming surfaces to reflect the club lights out onto the water.

Club *Sterling* was right. And Chris sure as shit didn't

have enough sterling in his bank account to be let in here. But he did have a shiny badge that got him past the bouncer, and once inside, he was grateful for the black dress slacks and collared shirt he'd dug out of the back of his closet. He was getting plenty of looks, but none of them were the you-don't-belong sort. They were the sort he might have returned for a chance at a quick fuck a few weeks ago, but now he ignored them and made his way to the bar instead.

"What'll it be, handsome?" the bartender asked, also giving him an appreciative once-over.

Fernet would be appropriate in a place like this, but he couldn't stand the bitter liquor. "Stout. Gravity, if you got it."

"I've got it," she said with a wink. "Be right back."

She headed to the other end of the bar, and Chris did a slow shift, from his left hip to his right, surveying the space, cataloguing the exits, and noting any variations from the blueprints he'd studied earlier.

"Here you go," the bartender chirped behind him.

Rotating back to the bar, Chris wondered at the items left on the napkin. The bottle of beer was correct, but the pair of eyeglasses next to it were unexpected. "I don't—"

"You left them last time you were here." She pushed the items closer and tapped a barely there bump under the napkin.

"Thanks for holding them for me," he said, acknowledging what was said and unsaid.

"No problem. Let me know if you need anything else."

He waited for her to move on to another customer

before he slipped on the tortoiseshell frames and lifted the bottle. Pretending the napkin was stuck to the bottom, he cupped his hand beneath it and caught the tiny comm unit. Bottle in one hand, he used the other to push back his hair and, in the process, tucked the comm into his ear.

"Good evening, da Vinci," Holt greeted.

Chris took a swig of beer, then with the bottle in front of his mouth, hiding its movement, whispered low, "We're sticking with that?"

"Efficiency."

"And the glasses?"

"Disguise, and the camera in them gives me a better view. Club floor is packed. I can't see everything through the security cams."

"So you're using me?"

"Yep," Holt said, not sounding the least bit contrite. "You're the designated observer."

"Where are you?" Not in the manager's office, Chris guessed. That would effectively put all three siblings in the same place. Too risky. But Holt would be close.

"Fire station." A building over, close but protected. "Now stop worrying about my twenty and do your job. Give me a good look around."

Chris took another swallow of the stout and repositioned himself, back to the bar, elbows resting on its rounded edge. He slowly panned the dance floor, giving Holt the requested look. It was hell on Chris, not focusing all his attention on locating Hawes, but the careful survey gave him the opportunity to locate several other familiar faces in the crowd—the Madigan captains from that morning and those he'd only ever seen on his office wall. They blended in expertly. If Chris didn't know any better, he'd think they were like the rest of the hipsters filling the club, young, rich, and out for a night on the town. But knowing what he did, Chris recognized their positioning for what it was—a Madigan operative on each exit and one in each quadrant of the dance floor.

And where the four corners met in the center of the room, Helena and Avery were putting on a show. Dancing close but with enough club light between them to be decent, barely. They moved in sync, with each other and the music, and their sexy show was drawing eyes from all over the club, including from Patrick McKennie.

"Van Gogh, Degas," Holt said, "you've caught the Irishman's eye. Up the ante."

The taller Avery draped her long brown arms over Helena's shoulders, bare above Helena's leather bustier, while Helena dove her hands into the back pockets of Avery's jeans, hauling her closer. Ante upped, indeed, and so much for decency. And so much for McKennie's date, assuming that's who the woman was in the booth next to him. His gaze was locked on Avery and Helena, eyes widening as Avery wove her fingers into Helena's long blonde hair, tilted back her head, and nuzzled her neck. That was the tipping point for McKennie, who brushed off his date and slid out of his booth. He wove through the crowd toward Helena and Avery, exactly as they'd intended. Chris hid his smile behind another drink from his bottle.

"Nine o'clock," Holt said.

Chris shifted his attention toward the wall of windows. Antonin Volz had his beefy arms slung over the shoulders of two girls, neither of whom looked a day over twenty-two, barely old enough to be in here at all. And definitely not old enough to realize the level of asshole they were flirting with. One of Volz's soldiers opened the terrace door, ushering Volz and his unsuspecting prey outside.

"Cézanne, Monet, you're up as soon as Matisse intervenes." On cue, Volz's rearguard got tangled up with Sue on the dance floor, which gave Alice and Victoria the chance to duck out after Antonin's party.

"Where's Rembra—" Chris didn't finish his question. Didn't need to. He'd swung his gaze forward and found the man he'd been searching for. Finally. Only he suspected everyone else had found him too. Dressed in combat boots, dark jeans, and a black tailored suit jacket, no shirt on underneath, Hawes slowly descended the stairs from the mezzanine. Like he wanted every set of eyes on him, like he owned the fucking place. The king in all his glory, no matter what anyone said. Top strands moussed for maximum volume, the sharp lines of his face were accentuated, as was the blue of his eyes, practically glowing in the club lights. Beautiful and dangerous, the picture of control, in his movements, his appearance, and his sway over the room.

Chris nearly choked on the need to shove his way through the crowd and meet Hawes at the bottom of the stairs, to claim the man as his, to give him the release from the control that Chris knew was costing Hawes so much when he had so little left to give. It ached—in his gut, in his chest, in his dick—to be even this far away from him.

"Stay at the bar," Holt said, as if reading his thoughts. The surprising snap of command in his tone shocked Chris back the step he'd taken toward Hawes. "Get it together."

Cursing, Chris drowned his instincts with the rest of his beer. "That's not exactly discreet."

"He's not meant to be. He's the distraction."

Fuck. Chris recalled what Hawes had said to him last week after the auction: *"If that's what it took to keep my family and city—you—safe."* He'd been willing to sacrifice himself then, same as he was willing to do now. So the rest of his team could do their work, and so he could prove to Remy Pak that he could still control a room. She was leaning over the mezzanine rail, watching as Hawes snaked through the crowd, pretending to eat up the attention, to respond to the hands on him and the propositions whispered in his ear. Hawes smiled indulgently at every suitor, and moved each one exactly where he wanted them, disguising his intentions with dips and sways to the music. Moving, with each interaction, closer to Ferriello's gathering. He caught the eye of two of Ferriello's men, who after a quick word with their boss, started toward Hawes.

"They're on him," Chris said, setting the empty bottle on the bar.

"Just wait," Holt warned. "Remember, he's the distraction."

And boy did Hawes play up his role, drawing Ferriello's men in with hungry eyes and a sexy smirk. Chris couldn't say if their initial interest had been business or pleasure, but Hawes's confidence, the sex appeal rolling off him, made the latter impossible for Ferriello's men to resist. Positioning one on either side of him, Hawes danced with the two men, dividing his attention equally, keeping them both on a string. Leaning his body into the one who wrapped an arm around his waist, under the flaps of his jacket, while turning his face toward the other, who was grinding on his hip. Keeping each soldier's holstered weapon on the side facing away from him and out toward the crowd, where a Madigan captain could quickly divest them. It was masterful, it was frustrating, and it was sexy as hell.

"Jesus Christ," Chris muttered, rotating back to the bar and flagging down the bartender. "Something stronger."

She smirked, sensing his conflict as any good bartender would do. Or she'd seen him adjusting himself. "You were the hottest piece of ass in here," she said, setting the generous shot of amber liquid in front of him, "until he walked in."

"No shit." Chris tossed back the shot of whiskey and let the burn refocus him.

"Feel better?" Holt asked.

"Marginally."

"Good. Now show me something else. Status on the other targets."

After a quick check on Hawes, who still had the undivided attention of Ferriello's guards, Chris searched out Avery and Helena. They were dancing on either side of McKennie, kissing over his shoulder until McKennie insisted on getting in on the action. They took turns kissing him, and by the time Helena was done with him, he was wobbly. And not just in the near-coital kind of way.

"They gave him something."

"To make him more pliable on the way to his long farewell," Holt said as Helena and Avery led McKennie toward the stairs.

"They've picked up a tail," Chris reported, tracking a McKennie guard on their heels.

"Remy's on him," Holt replied, and Chris looked up to find Pak making her way to intercept the guard. "Show-stopper appearing on your six."

From the kitchen doors behind the bar, Victoria and Alice emerged, now in server uniforms, carrying trays of champagne and cake. They made their way along the perimeter, heading for Ferriello's two party booths at the end.

"He getting a farewell present too?"

"His will be much shorter."

"Not if he doesn't eat or drink," Chris replied, watching with a sinking feeling as Ferriello brushed off the champagne and cake, his gaze instead trained on Hawes. "Looks like someone was too good a distraction."

Ferriello scooted out of the booth and made a beeline for Hawes, who was now sandwiched between Ferriello's guards. "Backup plan?"

"My brother is more than capable of handling this on his own."

"I know he is, but he shouldn't have to," he bit back. "I'm his partner, dammit!"

Silence greeted him, and the gravity of his words, the

truth of them, sank into the center of his chest. It could have thrown him for a loop, but it focused him instead, put this operation into tactical terms his brain could use to muffle his possessive heart.

"There are at least four other crews in this club," Chris said. "All of them with eyes on Hawes. And Ferriello is carrying."

"We have our operatives," Holt replied.

"None of whom are carrying, am I right?" He'd seen no telltale signs of holsters or guns on Alice and Victoria when they'd passed close by a moment ago, nor on Avery and Helena as they'd climbed the stairs with McKennie. He assumed the other captains had likewise foregone the firepower.

"You're not wrong," Holt confirmed.

A show of support for Hawes that Chris both appreciated and cursed. "Those other four crews are not as ethical."

"You're only there to observe. You don't have a gun on you either."

He didn't, but that was hardly the point. "What part of partner didn't you understand?" Chris dug a twenty out of his wallet, slapped it on the bar, and began cutting a path through the crowd to Hawes.

As if sensing the volcano about to erupt, Hawes lifted his chin, and his gaze shot past Ferriello's guard grinding against his front, past Ferriello himself, who was five seconds from ripping his guard out of the place he wanted to be, and clashed with Chris's.

Chris froze mid-step, a monolith as bodies jostled

around and into him. He hardly noticed them, having a silent conversation with Hawes instead. Partners—in life or work—trusted each other to make the right call. If Hawes wanted to handle this himself, Chris had to trust him. This was his call.

Hawes made it, with a come-hither smirk and inviting tilt of his head.

Chris answered the call. Coming unstuck, he forced his posture and his carriage into the casual, loping swagger that had started all of this. Tonight was another of those occasions when he needed to be Dante Perry, not Special Agent Christopher Perri. And thanks to Tran, who'd wisely not mentioned his name or flashed his picture at recent press conferences, no one seemed to recognize him as he cut across the dance floor.

"He's got a pill. Inner jacket pocket," Holt told him. "Five minutes, once it hits saliva."

"Copy that."

Two more steps and Chris was close enough to over-hear Ferriello say to Hawes, "Rumor has it you've returned to the dark side."

Grinning, Hawes slung his right arm over Ferriello's shoulder. "Don't believe everything you hear, Nicky."

Eyes flicking to Chris, Hawes made a circling motion with the hand behind Ferriello's head and tilted his own head slightly back. A signal. *Come around behind me.*

Chris continued to listen in as he moved into position.

"If it's true," Ferriello said, "we could fuck some shit up together. Wouldn't mind having some fun with the Prince of Killers."

Hawes shuddered, and Chris recognized the reaction for what it was—disgust and revulsion, a moniker Hawes hated but used when he had to, like in the present instance. Hawes smiled, playing his shiver off as attraction and excitement. "Not ruling it out," he answered coyly. "But that's not the kind of fun I'm looking for tonight."

"Aw, come on, Madigan," Ferriello said. "I wasn't around before you got all pious and shit."

"Oh, Nicky," Hawes cajoled, running a finger along the merc's jaw. "I'm a long way from pious."

Chris stepped directly behind Hawes and grasped his hip, spreading his fingers and squeezing, the gesture theirs, letting Hawes know it was him. "I can attest to that," Chris said, loud enough for Ferriello to hear. He cast a cursory glance at the other man, then nuzzled behind Hawes's ear.

"What's this?" Ferriello snapped, defensive at being challenged for Hawes's attention.

"*Who*, Nicky, and this is Dante Perry."

Chris smothered his grin in the crook of Hawes's neck. Partners, indeed.

"You with him?" Ferriello said.

"I am," Hawes answered.

"He is," Chris echoed, stretching his good arm around Hawes's shoulder, over his chest, and inside the opposite lapel of his jacket. A possessive gesture, and one that also gave him access to Hawes's inner pocket and the pill inside it. "I heard mention of some fun tonight. I'm game."

Ferriello's dark eyes flared. Definitely interested. Chris knew he and Hawes looked good together, knew they would be a temptation a playboy like Ferriello wouldn't be quick to dismiss.

Chris tempted him some more. "What else do you want to do with the Prince of Killers?" He drew Hawes firmly against his chest, then uncurled his arm from around him. Once clear, Hawes, with his arm still over Ferriello's shoulder, dragged the merc closer. Chris then skated his hand up Hawes's neck, using it to angle Hawes's face.

"This maybe?" he said to Ferriello before tilting Hawes's face and kissing him. Gentle and seductive at first, a show for Ferriello, then hungrily, craving the taste he'd missed since morning, the heat of Hawes's skin, the way that sharp body melted against his. Hawes groaned, acknowledgment and want, and an opening for the pill to slip from Chris's palm into Hawes's mouth. Officially on the clock, Chris reluctantly pulled back and found their audience hooked.

Olive skin flushed, breathing rapid, Ferriello stepped closer, a leg on either side of Hawes's left thigh. "Yeah," he panted, skating a hand up Hawes's chest and neck in a motion that mirrored Chris's. His eyes roved over Chris. "And I want you to watch."

Chris braced his right leg on the outside of Hawes's and wrapped an arm around his middle, under his jacket, flattening his hand against Hawes's tight stomach. "I'm not going anywhere," he said, moving their lower bodies to the music.

Ferriello swayed with them and brought his mouth to Hawes's.

Jealousy flared, hot and sharp, in the pit of Chris's

stomach, but it was quickly doused by observation and admiration. Hawes didn't respond to Ferriello's kiss the way he had to Chris's. His skin didn't heat, his weight didn't shift, his breath didn't quicken. No, this kiss was all tactical and executed to perfection. He toyed with Ferriello, giving him several light, teasing kisses that made Ferriello chase for more, before, hand in Ferriello's hair, Hawes sealed their lips in a deeper kiss. And transferred the pill from one mouth to the other.

Ferriello jerked back. "Hey, what's—"

Hawes slapped a hand over his mouth. "Just a little something to make it extra fun."

"Two incoming on your six," Holt radioed, and Chris drummed his fingers twice against Hawes's belly.

Hawes removed his hand and cupped Ferriello's cheek. "Heard you liked to have fun, Nicky. Consider it a birthday gift." He leaned forward and nipped Ferriello's ear.

Pretending to be dancing still, Chris shifted them so the incoming guards were at Ferriello's back, not his and Hawes's. "Have fun with us, Nicky."

"Boss!" a guard called out.

Ferriello lifted a hand and glanced over his shoulder. "I'm fine," he told his men. "We're just having fun." They moved a few paces back, not as far as Chris would have liked, but he didn't have time to dwell, his attention drawn back to Ferriello, who was pushing up on Hawes. He dragged his mouth along Hawes's neck to his ear. "I cheeked the pill, assholes," he said, then sharp eyes on Chris again, spit the pill at his chest. It bounced off Chris's collar, against Hawes's shoulder, then onto the floor at their feet. "Poison," Ferriello scoffed. "Fucking woman's weapon."

Hawes righted his head and sank back, more fully into Chris and separating them from Ferriello. "The strongest people I know are women."

The merc smiled, smug like he knew the best secret. And apparently couldn't keep it. "You know, Hawes, one of those women still wants you dead. A two-million-dollar contract went up tonight, on your head." He slid his hands up Hawes's chest, going for his neck. "And guess who's close enough to pull it off."

Holt's "Bitch" echoed Chris's "Fuck." Rose had set them—Hawes—up again. But there was no time to wallow in the anger of betrayal, not with Ferriello going for the kill. Knocking aside his hands and wrapping both arms around Hawes's torso, Chris yanked him back, out of Ferriello's immediate reach. Ferriello raised a hand to signal for his guards to converge and reached the other inside his suit coat for his gun.

"Lift!" Hawes shouted, and Chris shifted his own weight, planting his feet, lowering his center of gravity, and leaning back, lifting Hawes off the ground in front of him. Hawes swung his legs up in a scissoring motion. The first kick knocked the gun out of Ferriello's hand, the second knocked out Ferriello. The merc sank to the floor like a rag doll, which brought every guard's gun up on Hawes and Chris. And every one of them found their gun kicked away from behind, a Madigan operative having snuck up on them.

At which point, panic at the disco broke loose. The Madigan and Ferriello crews were engaged in hand-to-hand combat, McKennie's men caught on to their missing boss, and Volz's muscle scurried for the exits, thinking their boss gone already and not wanting to get caught in the melee.

Hawes sprang forward, out of Chris's hold, and spun to face him. "Go!" he shouted.

"Are you fucking kidding? I'm not leaving you."

"I can't keep you clean if you stay."

"And I can't leave my partner!"

Everything around them was chaos—people shouting, glass breaking, bodies hitting the ground—but Hawes's smile in that moment was radiant. It silenced the swirling chaos and any remaining conflict between Dante and Chris in Chris's head. They weren't separate entities. They were both here, right where he was supposed to be. With Hawes.

"Let's have some fun, then," Hawes said, giving him a quick, hard kiss, before spinning back around and engaging the nearest Ferriello guard. Chris fought at his side, working with Hawes to take them down in pairs, until, after they'd dropped their third set, they turned to find only Madigan operatives standing. The club had cleared out, what was left of McKennie's crew was cornered in a booth by Helena, Avery, and Victoria, and the rest of the dance floor was littered with Ferriello's guards.

Applause erupted from the far end of the space. "Well played," Remy said, descending the stairs with several of her soldiers behind her. Her gaze zeroed in on Chris as she approached their group. "And you, Agent Perri, willing to get your hands dirty now, I see."

He looped an arm around Hawes's waist. "Just needed the right incentive."

"Well, then, consider me incentivized too." Her playful tone vanished, as she shifted her attention to Hawes. "I'll get this cleaned up, and then I'll be in touch." She extended a hand to him. "I look forward to doing business with you, Mr. Madigan."

"Likewise," Hawes said, shaking her hand. "Until then."

She nodded, and Hawes signaled for the Madigan operatives to retreat. They scattered different directions—Helena, Avery, and Victoria out the exit beneath the stairs, a group out the terrace doors, another out through the kitchen. Chris and Hawes exited via the front door, side by side, and as soon as it shut behind them, he grabbed Hawes by the wrist and hauled him down to the shadowed promenade. He tossed the eyeglasses into the water, the comm units in after them, then pressed Hawes against the railing, caging him in. Hawes's relieved sigh was music to Chris's ears.

"Better?" he whispered against the skin of Hawes's neck. He kissed a path to the sharp hinge of Hawes's jaw, flattening his tongue over it and soothing away the last of the tension there.

"Almost," Hawes breathed, then conversely pushed him back.

A spike of worry hammered Chris, until Hawes used the space he'd created to unbutton his jacket and boost himself onto the railing. Jacket open, knees spread, eyes molten ice, Hawes was an invitation Chris hurried to accept, closing the distance between them again and capturing Hawes's lips in a searing kiss. Hawes wrapped him up in arms and legs, and Chris was awash in possibilities. Warm, sweaty skin to run his hands over, a hard cock to rut against, the mouth he wanted to feast on until the sun rose behind them.

"You in those glasses tonight about did me in," Hawes mumbled.

Chris spread his hands over Hawes's chest. "Says the man wearing no shirt under his tailored jacket." He coasted a hand up, into Hawes's hair, and dove south with the other, cupping Hawes through his jeans and pressing the heel of his palm against the erection there. It swelled in his hand. Fuck, all he wanted to do was yank open Hawes's zipper, go to his knees, and put his mouth on Hawes, suck him off right here under the stars, with the waves of the Bay lapping behind them.

"Fuck, Dante." Hawes pressed up into his hand, cock straining the fly of his jeans. "Need you to get me home and fuck me."

Chris didn't think he was going to make it that far, and he wasn't the least bit ashamed about that fact. He wanted Hawes, now. "I don't need to get you home to make us come." Curling a hand under Hawes's thigh, he hiked the leg higher, shifting their angle so he could rut against Hawes's taint while Hawes's cock ground into his abs. "Come for me right here, baby."

Their hips rocked faster, driving them higher, so close

to the edge. And then a ringtone cut through their ragged, grunted breaths, piercing the otherwise quiet night.

Not just any ringtone.

Braxton Kane's.

Lily.

Chris ripped out of Hawes's arms, panic freezing lust in its tracks. Hawes, equally alarmed, jumped off the rail and struggled to get his phone out of his pocket, his trembling hands making the task difficult. This—seeing Hawes shaking with fear for his niece—made Chris ache almost as badly for him as he had in the club, but it was a different sort of ache. The need to comfort and support his partner. He curled a hand around Hawes's neck and gently knocked his flailing hand away. "Breathe, baby, then try again."

A deep, shuddering breath later, Hawes managed to get the phone out of his pocket. Chris steadied his hand, the two of them holding the device together as Hawes hit Accept and put it on speaker. "Is she moving Lily?" he asked, voice cracking.

"No," Kane replied, and they each released a held breath. Only to have it stolen again at Kane's next words. "But Amelia just showed up at the house, with a bruised and bloodied Scotty Wheeler."

CHAPTER ELEVEN

"It was all a fucking diversion."

"Not completely true," Helena said, shifting in the passenger seat of the SUV. "It was also a show for Remy."

"An unnecessary one." Hawes stared out the rear window as the city flew by, Holt racing to get them to the house in Pac Heights. After getting a similar call from Kane, Holt had come barreling out of the fire station in the SUV, squealing to a stop at the curb to pick up Hawes, then a few blocks down the Embarcadero, Helena.

Traffic noise blared from the speakers, Chris switching off mute. "It wasn't unnecessary," he agreed. "Not to sell this."

"How the fuck am I supposed to sell that I kept Wheeler alive?"

"She respects power. That's how you have to spin it."

"Fuck!" Hawes braced his elbows on his knees and raked his hands through his hair, flattening the mousse-stiff strands. His hair was fucking ridiculous. This whole thing was fucking ridiculous. When were they ever going to get ahead of Rose? Was it even possible? Every time he thought they had the upper hand, Rose yanked the rug out from under them again. He'd had wins tonight: securing the captains' allegiance, Remy's cooperation, and Chris's declarations. But learning that Rose had put a contract out on him and that she'd kidnapped Scotty were two massive losses.

"When you get to the station," Holt said to Chris, who'd taken off in the opposite direction, "I want a report on Jax."

"Kane said they were fine. They weren't at the house when Scotty was taken."

"That doesn't mean they're fine," Holt replied. "Shelter kids are sensitive to things being taken from them. Wheeler being snatched out from under their nose might trigger some of those same fears."

"Got it," Chris said. "I'll make sure they're okay."

"We're at the house," Helena said as they rumbled onto the driveway pavers.

Hawes lifted his head, glancing out the front windshield at his childhood home, fearing it like he had haunted houses as a kid. Not that this house was dark; every main floor light and Holt's lair lights were blazing, but it was spooky—deadly, even—for other reasons.

"Kane still there?" Chris asked.

Hawes swiveled in his seat to look out the back window, to the same spot where they'd waited the night of the MCS showdown. The same dark cruiser was there now. "Yeah, he's still here."

"Tell him I'll meet him at the station," Chris said. "And keep me posted."

"Ten-four," Holt said, then clambered out of the car, heading Kane's direction without a second thought.

Helena exited at a more human speed, and Hawes took an extra minute to slip a T-shirt and loaded holster on under his jacket. How fucked up was it that he was fine walking into a club full of armed gangsters without a weapon, but he was unwilling to walk unarmed into his family home? He had no idea what surprises awaited him in there, and he wasn't willing to risk his siblings' or niece's lives. He composed himself, then climbed out of the car and waited with Helena at the back bumper.

Her attention was on their brother, who was leaning against Kane's driver's side door, speaking to the chief through the open window. "Should he—"

"It's fine," Hawes said. "Kane's safe."

Her attention swung to him, a brow raised in question.

"Part of the deal I made with Rose." Granted, their grandmother wasn't holding to the rest of the truce, but Kane's role was independent of Hawes, which Hawes hoped insulated the chief. But they couldn't push her too far. "His presence here tonight, though, is one more thing I have to explain."

She gestured toward Holt and Kane. "That one's easy, *if* she noticed." Then she pointed up at the house. "The other one, not so much."

"Chris is right. We'll spin it." He rested back against the bumper. "But how did she fucking find him?"

"Mr. Hair must have missed a tail. Or Jax."

Hawes shook his head. "I don't buy it."

"Neither do I."

"Do you have a file on you?"

"Do I look like a manicurist?"

Hawes held out his hand, palm up. She didn't go into an op without knives, as in multiple. Sure enough, she dug the blade out from between the seams of her bustier. "Thank you," he said, tucking it up his sleeve.

Across from them, Kane's car came to life, engine cranking and lights flashing on. Holt double tapped the hood, and Kane drove off, down the hill toward the station.

"He good?" Helena asked, once Holt had rejoined them.

"Not in the slightest, but he's Perri's problem tonight." He glanced up at the house, then back to Hawes and Helena. "How are we gonna play this?"

Hawes pushed off the bumper. "I have a starting point, spinning it as Chris suggested. We'll improvise from there."

"Haven't you improvised enough tonight?"

"Only as much as we had to to accomplish the mission *she* gave us. Which we did. No more tests. She wants to force our hand with Wheeler, then we'll force hers. I want this done."

"Agreed," Helena and Holt said together.

Did they still agree with him, however, once they reached the lair and got their first look at a tortured Scotty Wheeler? The agent was strapped to a chair in the middle of the room; Rose stood menacingly behind him.

"You want to explain to me why the dead fed is still very much alive?" she demanded.

"I needed information," Hawes answered. "From what Perri told me, Agent Wheeler is the best at finding it."

Rose circled the agent enough to see his face. "You agreed to help him?"

Narrow slits of brown, barely visible between bruised and puffy lids, shifted between Rose and Hawes. "I thought he was working for the good guys."

Hawes approached, risking Rose's striking distance to squat in front of Wheeler. And to drop the file on the floor by his left foot, out of Rose's eyesight. "You should have gone with that first instinct of yours."

Wheeler closed his eyes and gulped, selling it for Rose, as he moved his foot over the file.

"You were getting me the info I needed," Hawes continued, "and now we have a federal agent as leverage."

"As a hostage."

"I was trying to be kind."

"Fuck you," Wheeler spat.

"Was anyone working with you?" he asked, knowing Rose would if he didn't.

"No," Wheeler answered. Too fast. He was a desk jockey, not a field agent. How had he even survived Rose's torture this long?

Hawes peeked at Amelia out of the corner of his eye. She was sitting in Holt's chair in front of the bank of computers, Lily in her arms. Was she still on their side? How much had she told Rose about what she'd seen at Gillespie's property? She cuddled Lily closer. Was that a sign? Was she willing to play ball for the good guys if it got her more time with her daughter? Chris would tell him to trust her. Trusting him, Hawes squarely settled his gaze on Amelia. "Was he alone?"

"Yes."

Hawes slowly let his held breath out through his nose. Also seemingly satisfied with Amelia's answer, Rose headed for the couch. "What did you need him to find?" she asked him.

Hawes stood. "Information on the competition. And on Elliot Brewster."

Rose's steps faltered. He'd actually managed to surprise her. He followed her to the seating area and claimed an armchair. "You were willing to work with Reeves," he said, "to initially steal the explosives and move or sell them. When Reeves was eliminated, you moved on to your other partner. I wanted to know who that was, and you'd already been working with Brewster."

"You were supposed to trust me and do as you were told."

Not if he ever wanted her respect, or at least enough of it so she'd stop trying to kill him. Time to flex some of that power. "I don't blindly take orders, from anyone. Not when the lives of our family and our people are on the line. We make decisions together."

"And this decision, regarding Brewster... Do you disagree with me? With the direction?"

"I do disagree." Before she could object or let her speculation run rampant, Hawes carried on. "Because there's a better option on the table, and she's game. We passed your test and hers tonight. Now let's move the fuck on."

"What about the fed?" Rose said with a nod to Wheeler, who sat trembling in his chair. "You've got the information you needed."

"Doesn't mean he's not still leverage."

"And if I asked you to kill him?"

She'd posed that same question to him before, only then it had been about Chris, and Chris hadn't been in the same room. He couldn't answer differently now without giving away the ruse. He shifted in the chair and withdrew his gun, leveling it at Wheeler.

The agent's eyes widened, as much as they could before he winced, caught between fear, confusion, and pain. "Please, no."

"I'll do it," Hawes told Rose, "but I don't think it's the right call. Are you sure you can trust Tran?"

"She's the one who told us where he was."

Hawes was glad to be angled away from Rose right then. It covered his surprise. Whether it was a good one or a bad one, he wasn't sure. Either Tran had purposely sent him in, or Tran was actually dirty. And Wheeler couldn't signal him either way without signaling Rose. Didn't matter, though. Hawes's response to Rose was the same either way. "Holding him helps keep her in line. She hasn't said a word about him—missing or dead—for a reason. And he can give us more information on Perri, if we need to neutralize him."

"I think it's the right play," Helena said.

"Same," Holt added.

"Amelia?" Rose said.

His sister-in-law's green eyes flickered to him, then over his shoulder to Rose. "Holt and I can hack all day, but the fed can give us a more concrete direction to go in."

"All right," Rose said, after what felt like the longest five seconds of Hawes's life. "We'll play this one your way. You've earned that much."

Hawes allowed himself two seconds to fume over the backhanded compliment before he lowered his gun and rotated back around in his chair. "Thank you. Now, can we talk about how to finish this?"

"Interesting choice of words."

"I want to be finished with the doubts, and with the ATF, so our family can move on and thrive. Same as you."

She rose, and Hawes worried for a moment that he'd overplayed his hand. But then Rose held a hand out toward the stairs. "I've got the plans for the next phase laid out in the dining room."

He hadn't overplayed his hand at all. He'd played it just right.

Chris beat both Kane and Tran to the station, but not Jax. Their bike was parked in the back lot, the fender still warm to Chris's touch. The duty cop riding the night desk confirmed they'd arrived five minutes ago, and Chris hung a right at the top of the stairs, toward IT instead of Kane's office. He crossed the threshold and spotted Jax at their workstation, hanging their leather jacket on the back of their chair. Before he could speak, though, the burner in his pocket vibrated. He dug out the phone, read the text from Holt, and cursed.

"Guessing that wasn't good news," Jax said.

Chris glanced first at Jax, then at the other IT officer in the mini bullpen. His glare, fueled by the anger Holt's message had sparked, was enough to send the young man scurrying. Once he was out the door, Chris closed it behind him.

Jax collapsed into their chair. "Is it about Scotty? Is he okay?" They looked worn out and torn up, like they hadn't slept for days, and yet the nightmares had still caught up to them.

Remembering what Holt had said, Chris sat in the chair across from them and scrubbed the simmering anger from his voice. That ire was reserved for Tran, not Jax. "Hey, this wasn't your fault."

"He's a nice guy. I left... I didn't think..." They picked up a pencil and began bouncing the rubber end against the desk.

"Tran did this, not you. That's what Holt texted. That Tran was the one who sent him in."

His words seemed to make the guilt plaguing Jax worse, the pencil bouncing faster. "I think," they said, "that Scotty actually did this."

Chris shot to the edge of his seat. "He *what?*"

"We found a series of suspect cash transfers, but we need to be hooked directly into the Madigans' system to access the most recent ones, which is the last piece we need to tie Rose to Brewster and the explosives... And to Isabella."

Fucking hell, *now* Scotty wanted to play cowboy?

"I'm sorry," Jax said. "I should have realized and stopped him."

"Listen to me, Jax. This isn't your fault. He went in with his eyes open. That's good."

"She could still kill him."

Chris reached out and laid a hand over theirs, stilling the pencil. "We'll get him back. For now, we're gonna have to trust Hawes, Helena, and Holt to keep him alive. You trust them, don't you?"

"I'd trust them with my life."

"Then trust them with Scotty's."

They took a deep breath and laid down the pencil. "All right."

Before either of them could say anything more, Chris's other phone buzzed with a **Where are you?** text from Kane. He tapped back an **On my way** as he stood and turned toward the door. "Let's go fill them in and plan a rescue."

"Wait!" Jax said. They rounded the desk, a flash drive in hand. "This is everything we found about the night Isabella died, including the missing footage from the scene." They held out the flash drive, and Chris took it warily, as if it might bite. And then they went and doubled the fun, holding out a second flash drive, this one with a sheet of paper folded around it. "And I think maybe this is the last piece of the story."

He recognized the slip of paper. On the outside, in Tran's handwriting, was the name of Remy's captain. Except, as he unfolded it from around the flash drive, he saw the writing on the inside too. *I'm trusting you, Dante,* in a different hand.

"Where did you get this?" Chris asked.

"It was on the table when I got back to the house and Scotty was gone."

Amelia had been the one to bring him to the house in Pac Heights. Chris wasn't familiar with her handwriting, but he guessed he was looking at it right then. She was trusting him to do what? The right thing with whatever was on this drive? Or more than that? Her note was on this paper for a reason. She was trusting him to uphold the bargain they'd made in the transport van this—yesterday— morning. To do right by her and her family for her coopera- tion. And what? She was giving him the rest of the answers now? On this drive?

"Did you check what's on it?" he asked Jax.

They shook their head. "It was clearly for you."

The urge to log on to any of the dozen computers in here to see what was on the second drive was damn near irresistible.

Wait for Hawes, Izzy said in the back of his head, her voice returning from wherever it had disappeared to the past few days. *Watch it with him.*

She was right. If whatever was on this flash drive was anything like the video on the first one of Amelia's they'd found, he didn't want to watch it alone. He'd seen Holt's and Helena's immediate reactions after watching that one and Hawes's reaction at the condo when he'd nearly torn it apart. Hawes shouldn't have been alone the first time he'd watched it. Chris wouldn't be alone this time. And he wanted it to be Hawes with him.

He folded the paper back around the second drive and pocketed it. "Is there anything on here"—he held up the first drive Jax had handed him—"that Kane and Tran shouldn't see?"

"No, it's mostly financials and the incident footage," Jax said, gathering up their laptop and files.

"All right, then. Let's go."

They reached Kane's office and found the chief squaring off against Tran. "You didn't think to tell us you were sending him in?"

"Agent Wheeler called me," Tran said. "He told me he needed inside the Madigan compound, and I had an hour to extract him."

"Amelia would have been closest," Chris said, announcing their presence.

Kane hardly acknowledged them, his wrath still directed at Tran. "Why did he need inside?"

"I can answer that," Jax said. They opened their laptop on Kane's desk and logged on to a secure server. "Right now, we only have Amelia directly tied to the explosives, and she's not our ultimate target. So Scott—Agent Wheeler —and I were following the money, trying to connect Rose more directly to trafficking in explosives, as that's the ATF's jurisdiction." They opened an account ledger. "We flagged this separate trust account Rose set up for Lily. There were irregularities that stood out from the other trust accounts set up by Hawes, Holt, and Helena." They toggled to side-by-side spreadsheets, one showing deposits, the other withdrawals. "We back traced the account that made these deposits into the trust." They highlighted those green. "And the account that received these payments." They highlighted those red.

"Payments, from the trust account?" Kane said. "Lily's eight months old. There shouldn't be any payments."

"Exactly. And they're all going, through a series of transactions, to the same entity, which has an account set up at the same offshore bank we previously flagged."

"That's gotta be Rose," Chris said.

"And the numbers match," Tran noted. "The money came in and went back out in the same amount."

Chris connected the dots. "She was using the trust account to funnel the money for her coup."

Jax nodded. "Separate from any other Madigan accounts."

"And that's why she needed Amelia. To disguise the transactions and hide the money trail."

"How do you know it's connected to the explosives?" Tran asked.

Jax clicked on several of the green-highlighted deposits, then on the amount cells of the first two. "Add these two up. Does that sum ring any bells?"

"Yes!" Kane said, tearing apart the stacks of files and papers on his desk. His prize was a thin manila folder near the bottom. He opened it, revealing a single sheet of paper —the ad for the dark web auction. Kane pointed at the buy-in amount. "It's the sum."

"Exactly," Jax said. "Now, that money came into the trust from this entity, which also made these two other deposits." They clicked on the other green entries they'd highlighted.

"Let's assume this"—Chris pointed at the entity making the deposits—"is Brewster."

"We're ninety-nine percent certain it is, given the account's other activity and the corporate formation documents. We just need a warrant to get the Account Control Agreement."

"Give me everything you've got on this account and on Rose's," Tran said. "I'll take care of the warrants."

"Thank you," Chris said, then asked Jax, "Are there matching payments out for these deposits?"

Jax toggled over to the payment screen again. "For three of them."

Three of them, Izzy prompted. *Not four.*

Why not four? Chris reread each highlighted line.

What's important about those amounts? Izzy asked.

The first two were the same—together, the total auction amount—and then the other two were the same, albeit significantly larger sums. Two sets.

Installments.

Made how often?

The dominos began to fall in Chris's head. "Look at the dates," he said, reaching an arm over Jax's shoulder. He tapped the date on the auction deposit. "That's the down payment for the auction." He pointed at the same payment a day later. "And that's the rest of it, for getting the job done."

"But Hawes didn't die in that auction," Tran said.

"He didn't," Chris conceded. "But he removed one of Brewster's competitors, and Rose proved she had the explosives."

"So then this"—Kane tapped at the earlier, larger installment on the date of Callum's funeral—"is the first payment for the explosives?"

Chris nodded. "When Rose first stole them."

"And that's the second," Tran said, identifying the last. "Made yesterday, for when she delivers them. But she hasn't paid it back out of the trust account yet."

"Because of Remy?" Kane asked. "Because she's not sure she'll deliver them to Brewster now?"

"Or," Jax said, "because there's a delay in the bank showing it. They're down for maintenance at this time of night, but if we're in her system..."

"You can see if the action has been scheduled," Chris said, putting it all together. "And if she's still planning to proceed with Brewster." He rounded on Tran, another realization hitting him. "We could have not risked Scotty and trusted Amelia to confirm this."

"I didn't," she said. "And I wasn't taking any chances. That's why the timing was imperative. Rose has been paid for the job. If that money is paid out, she'll steal those explosives right out from under their—*and our*—noses."

"No *if* about it," Jax said. "Scotty just sent us a message."

All eyes swung to them, and to the text box open on their screen.

Two words: **payment scheduled.**

CHAPTER TWELVE

"That's the plan," Hawes said, looking up from the break room table he stood beside. It was covered with maps and satellite photos, a route marked on each. Five hours from now, just after rush hour, an ATF transport driven by Tran and Chris would travel that route, moving the seized explosives from evidence lockup to a controlled detonation facility, ironically only a couple of miles from where they now stood, in the warehouse where the weapons were manufactured and stored. "Everyone understand their roles?"

Various points along the route had been circled. The plan Rose had laid out for him, and which Hawes had relayed to their operatives, included locations where the Madigans were supposed to intercept the transport, where a third party might beat them to the intercept and attempt a rip-off, and where they were supposed to transfer the explosives to Remy.

Hawes, together with Chris, Tran and Kane, had subsequently added locations where a handoff to Brewster was more likely to occur, where Rose might try to steal the explosives for herself, and where SFPD and the ATF would have secondary teams. Law enforcement would be less than a quarter mile from each other identified location, ready to converge on their signal. They would allow the handoff to occur—either to Remy, who had made a verbal agreement with Rose for the weapons, or to Brewster, whose account agreements would show he'd paid for them —thereby solidifying the trafficking charge against Rose. If she tried to steal them for herself, with force, they'd have her on grand theft robbery, plus theft of evidence, obstruction of justice, and a whole host of other charges. Either way, once criminal action was taken, law enforcement would move in, seize the weapons, and make the arrest. Hawes had no delusions it would run so smoothly, but at least it was an elegant plan. Especially considering it had been conceived on no sleep at three in the morning.

"All set, boss," Avery said. She'd be driving the car with him in it, trailing the transport van.

Connor spoke next. "And I'll back up Kane on Rose." Rose and Amelia, who was supposed to be back in custody by mid-afternoon, would be at the house in Pac Heights, operating as base command. "We'll make sure she doesn't slip free."

That had been Hawes's one alteration to the assignments Chris had originally suggested. Kane was supposed to be the LEO on Brewster, but Hawes had shifted him to Rose. He was the one LEO in the least danger from her.

Though Hawes couldn't be certain she'd keep that promise, so he wouldn't leave Kane without backup.

Across the table from Hawes, Alice snapped pictures of the maps and photos, then handed the phone to Victoria. She quickly scrolled through them. "We're good," she said with a nod. "We'll get orders to the rest of the captains."

Hawes braced his hands on the back of the plastic chair in front of him. "Last chance," he said, meeting the gaze of each operative. "I'm giving you the same choice I did at the club. You and the other captains outnumber the four of us." Chris and Helena stood on either side of him, and Holt was listening in by phone. "Do you want to do this?"

"She put us through a needless test at Sterling," Victoria said. Before explaining the tactical, Chris had filled them in on the accounts Jax and Wheeler had discovered, the proof that Rose still intended to sell the explosives to Brewster. "She lied to us."

"So did I," Chris said.

Alice tilted her head toward Hawes and Helena. "They didn't." Her blue eyes landed on Hawes. "You made your rules clear."

"And you fought with us tonight," Connor said to Chris. "For Hawes."

"I intend to keep doing so." His hand landed in the center of Hawes's back, and Hawes felt its heat through the cotton of his tank, imagined it chasing away the chill that had gripped him since that call from Kane.

Connor nodded. "We know who we're standing

behind."

"And what we're standing for," Victoria added.

"All right, then." Hawes straightened, and Chris's hand drifted to his lower back, settling there, settling him. "Go home. Get a few hours of sleep if you can."

The operatives exited the break room into the main warehouse, Hawes and Chris trailing. Their steps boomed in the cavernous building, the sparse furnishings—the table and chairs in the break room, desks in the handful of offices, workbenches with scattered parts down the center of the A-frame's open space—doing little to muffle the echoes off glass, steel, and concrete. It reminded Hawes of a fucking tomb. He bet the storerooms where they had kept the explosives were even more creepy. Good riddance to that inventory, if only Hawes could actually be rid of it.

"Change of plans," Helena said from behind them. "I'm on the primary intercept team."

Hawes spun, nearly knocking Chris over in his haste to shut this idea down as fast as possible. "No fucking way."

"Why not?"

"Because when this is done, you're the fucking queen." The words were out before he could stop them. Before he could consider the full weight of them or discuss them with Chris. Not that they weren't true. Not that Hawes's thoughts hadn't been headed this direction already. Not that the overwhelming sense of pride and relief in saying them aloud hadn't suffused him with as much warmth as the hand at his back.

Helena caught her balance against the nearest work-bench, her big blue eyes staring back at him, shock and no small amount of fear swirling there. She looked much the same as she had in that courtyard after Papa Cal had died, except now the dark surrounded them instead of sunlight. And here again, it was as fitting a coronation as Hawes could imagine.

Hawes pointed toward the door where the operatives had left the building. "They were here because of *you*. Same as they were in the club. They trust *you*. They follow *you*."

She shook her head, not wanting to believe what he was saying. He half expected her to cover her ears with her hands. "That's not what I was after."

"I know," Hawes said, and Chris gave him a slight nudge forward. Taking the cue, Hawes reached out and squeezed his sister's shoulder. "And that's why it should be you leading them when the dust settles."

"What are you going to do?" She shrugged off his hand, some of the litigator fighting back and infusing her voice. "Fuck off with him somewhere?" she said with a flick of her hand at Chris. "Because that's not how this works. You, Holt, and I run this company, and the organization, together. That's what we've been fighting for."

"I might fuck off for a week with him, to fuck," Hawes said, trying to lighten the mood and earning the eye roll he wanted. "But after that, I'm back by your side," he assured her. "You're right. We do this together, and someone is going to have to step into Rose's role, making the social and political connections the company and organization need to survive."

Her lips rounded into an O, finally seeing what he had. The more natural fit for him in the evolved Madigan empire. "The alliances you've made..."

Hawes nodded. "Let me do what I'm good at, positioning us externally through the company and otherwise. You do what you're good at, which is organizing and leading us internally. And Holt will continue to be the technical engine that keeps us running."

She crossed her arms and furrowed her brow, contemplating, which was better than outright refusing. "We'll need to clear this with Little H."

Heat hit Hawes's back as Chris reached an arm around him and set his burner phone, face up, on the nearest bench, the call to Holt still connected. "Let's see what he says."

Helena gasped. "You kept him on the line?"

"Your own trick."

"It's the right move," Holt said. "Every aspect of it makes sense."

"And what about you?" Helena asked Chris.

"Seems your organization is the sort that could use a private investigator." His hand returned to Hawes's back, and Hawes never wanted to go without that touch. Chris's suggestion made it all the more possible. "I'm with him, in whatever capacity you all need," Chris said.

Helena's gaze shifted between them and the phone, as if she could somehow see Holt through it too. Eventually, she conceded, fighting with her topknot as she did. "I'm definitely not going to sleep tonight."

Hawes gently lowered her arm and cupped her shoulders. "One step at a time, Hena. You're not intercepting the truck, agreed?"

"Agreed, but if you need back up, I'm far away."

"Fair enough. We'll get through this op, through today, and then we can worry about the day after," he said, desperately hoping there was a tomorrow for all of them.

"He puts on a brave front, but—"

"But he's barely holding it together," Chris said, finishing Helena's sentence. He had witnessed Hawes's shaking hands during Kane's call, had heard the cracks in his voice after, had felt the tiny trembles that continued to intermittently ripple through Hawes.

Helena slung a leg over her Ducati. "Take care of him."

"Count on it." The helmet was just over her head when Chris recalled something else he'd meant to ask. "Why does he think Kane is safer on Rose?"

"Not totally. Connor is providing backup."

"That doesn't answer my question."

"He made a deal with Rose," Helena said. "It was his condition for breaking out Amelia."

"Because of Holt."

She nodded. "You hear from your family?"

"Safe and sound at the cabin," he said with a smile,

translating *family* to *Celia*. "Thanks for taking care of them."

She couldn't get the helmet on quick enough to hide her smile.

Chris's grin lingered as he walked back into the warehouse, until he glimpsed Hawes's solitary form at the far end of the space. Right arm braced above him, he was leaning against the windows, staring out at the Bay. Except as Chris approached, as Hawes's reflection in the glass resolved, Chris saw that Hawes's eyes were closed. Above them, his brow was pinched and his forehead wrinkled, and below them, his lips were pressed together in a thin line. Distress was similarly reflected in the tense curve of his spine and the fingers he dug into his hip, knuckles white.

"Hey," Chris said softly, warning of his approach. Hawes's eyes opened, the harsh lines of his face easing. Chris slid a hand under his, picking it up off his hip and holding it in his own as he wrapped Hawes in an embrace from behind. "You put on a good show just now, but you can talk to me."

Hawes didn't dodge the comment; further evidence of his exhaustion. "I don't want it to all be for nothing."

"No one fights this hard for nothing."

"I didn't really expect my grandmother to ever trust me again, but to have it confirmed like this..." Hawes lowered his arm and leaned fully back into Chris, head resting on his shoulder. "Forced into a battle of wills, of power, that could cost people their lives. I just want to do right by my family, by my city, by my people." He buried his face in Chris's neck. "And by you and the past."

By me, Izzy supplied, and Chris stiffened, remembering the flash drives in his pocket.

Hawes turned in his arms and reversed, thinking Chris's tension was something he'd caused. "What is it?"

Chris didn't let him get away. "Scotty and Jax didn't just find information on Rose's current activities."

"Her past ones too? Her involvement with Izzy's death?"

"Jax thinks so, and they recovered the video footage of the incident."

Face awash with remembered pain, Hawes did escape this time, wrenching out of Chris's arms and pressing himself back against the windows. "Did you watch it?"

Chris shook his head. "I didn't need that distraction right now. Which was the same reason why I didn't hand it over to Tran." He withdrew the second flash drive from his pocket. "Or give her this one."

Hawes paled impossibly further. "What's on that one?"

"Amelia left it for me when she took Scotty. After her last present, seeing what it did to you and your siblings, I didn't want to watch whatever's on here alone."

Hawes's gaze skipped toward the adjacent offices. "There's a computer still in one of those." He made no effort to move in that direction, though.

Neither did Chris. Instead, he crowded Hawes against the window, front to front, his right forearm braced over his head, not letting him escape. "I'm not sure we can handle what's on that drive on top of everything else."

"What if it's something we need to know?" Hawes whispered, like it was the very last thing he wanted to ask but had no choice.

"What if it's something meant to throw us off?" Chris countered.

"I thought you said Amelia is on our side."

"Can we be sure of that?"

"Of course not." Hawes closed his eyes and rested his head against the glass, fatigue overwhelming him once more.

Chris wished he could alleviate it, wished he could fast-forward through the events to come later that morning and be done with all of this. Arrest Rose now and skip the risky part altogether. But those were not the cards they'd been dealt. The best they could do was solve one problem at a time. The best he could do, in *this* moment, was try to ease Hawes's distress. He brushed the falling top strands off his forehead. "Let's not add more pieces to the already crowded board."

Chris glided his hand down, cupped Hawes's cheek, and Hawes nuzzled into the touch. "But isn't this the battle that matters most to you? What this has been about for you all along?"

Chris lightly grasped his chin and righted his gaze. Hawes opened his too blue eyes, and they were a cyclone of regret, weariness, determination, and desire, spinning so fast it would drown Hawes unless Chris could give him some peace in the storm. "This stopped being about vengeance for me a while ago."

"She deserves justice."

"And she'll get it, when we put Rose behind bars."

"Is that enough for you?" His Adam's apple bobbed as he swallowed hard.

Chris soothed it with his thumb. "You're enough for me."

"Even after the hell my family has put you through, is still putting—"

Chris silenced the rest of his words and the self-recriminations bubbling up from the floor of Hawes's emotions. Showing him instead what this had become about for him. The lips under his, the tongue sliding against his own, the sharp, stubbled jaw beneath his palms, and the tight, hard body between his and the window.

The heart beating in time with his.

Breaking the kiss, Chris rested his forehead against Hawes's, the other man's face in his hands. "You made me feel at home for the first time since Ro died."

"Dante."

Chris smiled so wide, it hurt his face. "And then there's that."

"I don't understand how, after what I did."

"You say it like you're lucky, like you think you still don't deserve it." Chris traced his thumbs through the wetness under Hawes's eyes. Through the evidence of the assassin's soul. "You do, baby. You make your family better, this city better, me better. And I want to make a home here, with you."

"You hardly know me. I've lied—"

"So have I." He hadn't denied it to Hawes's operatives, and he wouldn't deny it to the man himself. But it wasn't the entire story. "We've both lied, but the things that mattered were true." He removed a hand from Hawes's face and laid it over his heart. "I know you here." He trailed the hand lower, over his cock, which had stiffened against Chris's thigh as they'd kissed. "And here."

Chris stroked up and down Hawes's erection, which grew harder in his hand. He knew he was playing dirty, but he was on the cusp of winning this debate—the last time he wanted to have it. He needed Hawes confident going into this op, feeling like the king he was, and the fact that Chris could give that to him, that truth, mattered too. That part had never been a lie.

"That night in your condo against the ladder, when you gave me control of you, what mattered more—that you hardly knew me, or that I could give you this?" Chris pressed harder against Hawes, pinning him to the window, shoving his thigh between Hawes's legs.

Hawes keened. "Fuck yes."

"Or the times we've been together since. In my condo when I fed you my cock. The other morning in your bed." Chris kissed him, slow and deep, until they were both panting. "Does it make any difference to you that I don't know what your favorite color is? Or what your favorite food is?" Chris slowly sank to his knees. "Or does it matter that I make you feel steady?"

"Oh God," Hawes groaned, thrusting forward as Chris worked open his fly. "I need you."

Chris yanked Hawes's jeans and boxers down and breathed against the cock straining toward him. "I need you too, baby. In my mouth, in my home, in my future." He shifted back on his haunches and stared up at a lust-drunk Hawes Madigan. Hands on Hawes's hips, Chris pressed Hawes's bare ass against the window, breaking his daze enough to make him loll his head forward, gazing down at Chris. "Do you want that too, with me?"

"Fuck yes," Hawes moaned again. "All of it."

"Then trust me. Trust this as much as I do."

Chris expected an *okay*, an *I do*, a *yes*. He didn't expect Hawes to step out of his jeans and boxers and slink down the window onto his knees, bringing them front to front. To give Chris a long, claiming kiss, the best of Chris's life. He didn't expect Hawes to draw gently back with a "thank you" and then lie back on the floor, completely open for the taking.

Trusting.

Chris rewarded that trust. Teasing his cock and balls with licks and kisses. Nipping his way back up Hawes's body as he rid him of his tank, flattening his tongue over his nipples, sucking and biting and making Hawes's spine bow. Spreading Hawes's legs and ass cheeks and working him open with his tongue. And once Hawes was good and slick, writhing and begging for more, pumping his fingers in and out as he jacked Hawes's cock with his other hand. Leaning over and catching the eruption in his mouth as Hawes's chants of "I love you, I love you, I love you" echoed off the walls.

Then, once Hawes had caught his breath, Chris falling

onto the floor next to him and trusting Hawes to handle him with the same care. Arching his back and scrabbling at the unforgiving floor as Hawes mercilessly teased, kissed, and licked, then shouting as Hawes swallowed him down without preamble, confident and in control. Returning the chorus of "I love you, I love you, I love you" as his king sucked him off to the light of the morning sun streaming in through the windows and brightening their world.

CHAPTER THIRTEEN

E legant only lasted as far as the San Mateo Bridge. They had just crested the mid-rise and were coming down into Foster City when not one but two tails fell in behind them.

"We've got company," Hawes said. "Two bikes behind us."

"Bogey at the turnoff," Chris radioed. He was a few car lengths ahead, riding passenger in the transport van while Tran drove. "Black Jeep Trackhawk. Tinted windows. Can't detect the number of bodies inside."

The tails were unexpected, the bogey was not. This was one of the third-party rip-off spots they had anticipated. A spot where highway patrol frequently hid to speed-trap drivers who hadn't slowed down after coming off the bridge. A spot where someone aiming to highjack the van full of explosives could dart right out of.

Fuck, they weren't even going to get to where Alice

and Sue were supposedly hijacking the transport. Someone else was doing it first.

"Intercept four," Holt announced to the rest of the team, deducing the same. "Initiate traffic break at 101 and on the bridge at the rise. No more traffic coming through. Perri, slow enough for the traffic around you all to clear out."

But not so much that the tails behind them would catch up. It was a tricky balance. Avery, driving the vehicle Hawes was in, slowed to keep pace. At least whatever hell was about to break loose would be contained to this stretch of only a few miles. Didn't make the knot in Hawes's gut loosen much. Yes, he was ready to get this over with. Yes, he'd directed other complicated ops before, including the one last night. But none of those ops had this much riding on it—the lives of those he loved, the future of their organization, his family's legacy. He'd be a fool not to feel some apprehension.

"Clear of surrounding vehicles," Holt said.

Beside Hawes, Avery stepped on the gas, moving closer to the transport van. And Chris.

"Any idea who?" Hawes asked.

Holt, who was operating remote command in a Jax-driven van a mile ahead of the transport, was tapped into the traffic cams, full access courtesy of SFPD. "Can't get a read on the bikes' plates. Will get the Jeep's plates as soon as it hits the freeway."

Was this a true third-party rip-off, or Remy or Brewster springing early, or Rose trying to take off with the explosives while keeping Brewster's money? All options were on the table. Any of them could hijack the van, keep driving west on 92, hit 280, and be home free. Which was why they had planned for this scenario as well. They were ready.

More than ready. Fuck it. "Faster, Chris. Let's get this done."

Chris had the gall to chuckle. "Your patience is for shit."

"For this, it is. We've controlled the variables as much as we can. Let's do this, on our terms."

"Roger that."

Hawes heard the lingering smile in his voice, and it steadied him, even as the bikes behind them grew louder, speeding up too. "You ready to drive like our lives depend on it?" he said to Avery.

Her grin was positively ecstatic. "Always, boss."

"Three minutes out," Helena said over the roar of her Ducati.

"Hena," he warned, a reminder of their conversation last night.

"Backup only, I know."

"Victoria, Malik," Holt said, "confirm position."

"In position," Victoria replied. They were waiting just past the turnoff, in a parking lot near where the mileage sign overhung the freeway, a hole cut through the wire fence so the SUV they were in could plow through and enter the freeway if needed.

"Bogey is on the move," Tran said.

As were the bikes behind them, drawing up on either side of Hawes's rear bumper. "Faster, Avery."

Chris started the countdown ahead. "Passing the intercept point in three...two..."

"Fuck!" Holt shouted. "I've lost eyes on!"

And on the heels of that report, Chris bit out, "Jesus Christ!"

Hawes whipped around in his seat, looking ahead to where the bogey had charged onto the freeway right in front of the transport. The van swerved to avoid hitting the Jeep but clipped its back fender and sent it spinning. The van careened the opposite direction, teetering on two wheels, then came down hard, one tire blowing out with a bang.

Hawes caught sight of Chris's wide brown eyes for a split second before Avery shouted, "Incoming eastbound."

Hawes whipped his gaze to the other side of the freeway. Two sedans were drifting across the lanes, sliding so they'd align right on the other side of the dividing barrier. It would be a short hop over the concrete half wall and across a lane of traffic to where the transport had shuddered to a stop.

Hawes pointed ahead, to the gap. "Get between them."

"Can't go that direction. Bike's between me and the wall." Sure enough, the tail on their left had drawn up alongside the back door. And they were both closing in too fast on the van to just smash the bike into the wall. They wouldn't fit.

Hawes drew several knives out of the bag at his feet. Wrapping his nonthrowing arm through the seat-belt strap, he leaned out the car window, aiming for the bike on their right first, eliminating the other rider's cover. Two knives—

one into the driver's chest, the other into his front tire—and the bike and rider went down. He climbed farther out, ass on the window frame, and aimed toward the other rider. The first throw ricocheted off the rider's shoulder, slowing them down enough that Avery drew ahead, and Hawes got enough distance to hit the rider center mass with his next throw.

No sooner had he let the knife fly than Avery yanked him back into the car. He fell into his seat, and he could swear his right hand scraped metal as Avery drove them into the gap, swerving and wedging them to a grinding halt. An added barrier for the unrecognizable mercs climbing out of their cars.

"This way!" Knife in one hand, Hawes threw open his door with the other, and Avery climbed out after him, her door jammed against the barrier.

A shot flew overhead, Hawes and Avery ducked behind their vehicle, and then the roar of a bike Hawes knew well sounded not just over his comm. "I'm on them," Helena said.

Hawes turned, looking back through the window, and watched as a knife flipped end over end, lodging in the chest of the merc half over the wall. Helena didn't even slow, just kept bearing down on the other merc, who was now running the opposite direction.

Toward where two more cars were careening over the mid-rise of the bridge.

"Holt!" Hawes called. "We need eyes, ASAP! They keep coming! Malik, get back there for rear support!" He needed to get to where he could hear Chris and Tran engaged in combat, but he couldn't leave them exposed back here.

"On my way," Malik replied, while Holt continued to curse.

"She's fucking locking me out."

"Who?" Hawes said.

"Amelia! I can recognize my own code."

Hawes's blood ran cold.

This was Rose. Again.

Except these were hired mercs attacking them. Not soldiers.

He glanced again at the car descending the rise. Eva's. And was that another soldier in the passenger seat? Were they coming to attack or support? Helena's tires squealed, smoking, as she wheeled back around. Leaving her back exposed to the incoming cars. Because she knew who those belonged to. Who they were loyal to.

Same as the sirens that now joined the cacophony of noise. The cavalry was closing in too.

They had the numbers.

They had Rose.

And Hawes was so done with this shit.

Knife at the ready, Hawes stood and stalked across the freeway toward Chris, who was engaged in hand to hand with another merc. Catching sight of him, Chris kicked his attacker back, right into Hawes. Looping an arm around the merc's chest, Hawes sliced the knife across his throat, dropping the merc.

There was a merc at Tran's feet too, but her focus was

on the Jeep. "There's another one in there," she said, holding her gun at the ready. "I'm on it."

Hawes took his eyes off Tran for one second. One second to sweep his eyes up and down Chris, to check for any injuries, and in that one second, a shot rang out.

Tran's body spun, the force of the bullet sending her to the ground. "Tran's hit!" Chris shouted as he grabbed Hawes and yanked him behind the van.

"Victoria," Hawes called. She was the operative closest to Tran. "Get her clear."

"On it."

"We need to see who's in that car," Chris said, and Hawes nodded. Chris signaled to Avery to cover them, and he and Hawes approached together, Chris in front with his gun at the ready.

"ATF. Get out of the car."

Chris took another step toward the Jeep and a shot flew out the open back window. Hawes grabbed Chris by the back of the shirt and hauled him down, just in time.

"It's Scotty!" came Holt's panicked voice over the comm. "It's Wheeler in the car!"

"Are you sure?" Chris said.

"Amelia's blocking my eyes, but she sent me a message in the code."

Hawes hardly heard them, their back and forth no match for the blood rushing in his ears. Déjà vu of the worst kind washed over him, his worst nightmare come to life again. He saw the scene through his eyes of three years ago, something he'd fought to block out, same as he fought to control the variables in this op today, three years later.

Today was different. Light instead of dark. Dry instead of rainy. No gun in his hand, versus the Colt 1911. Yet it was the same. His future, his life, versus an innocent's.

The back door of the Jeep swung open, and bloodied wrists appeared, a gun in Scotty's hands, the bracing one missing a finger.

Calm resignation—and acceptance—washed over Hawes. It had never really been over, but it would be today, one way or the other. "Chris, back up."

"Hawes, no!" Chris shouted as Hawes moved in front of him.

Scotty wobbled on unsteady legs, tears streaming down his face as blood dripped from his wrists and hands. "I don't want to shoot you."

"I know," Hawes said, taking another step toward him.

On his periphery, Hawes saw Chris lower his gun and raise one hand. "Scotty, put down the gun."

"I can't! She caught me sending that message. Caught me trying to leave." He wheezed between heavy, labored breaths. "And she knows about Sam. She knows where Sam is! She's going to..."

"We won't let anything happen to Sam."

"You can't know that."

"Scotty," Hawes said calmly, drawing the agent's attention off Chris. He pointed at his chest.

Chris grabbed at his other arm. "Hawes, no, please."

"It's all led back to here, Dante."

"What part of don't sacrifice yourself—"

Hawes glanced over his shoulder, meeting dark, terrified eyes. "I understood. All of it. I also understand this can't end any other way." And it would seal the charges on Rose. No one in his family would ever be hurt again.

"Hawes, please." Barely a whisper, the last word cracking and cracking open Hawes's heart with it.

"I love you," he said. "Now trust me." He held Chris's gaze as he tugged his arm free.

Chris let it go, like making his fingers unclench was the hardest thing he'd ever had to do, and Hawes supposed if it were him in Chris's position, it would be for him too. "I love you too." Chris lowered his gun the rest of the way, and Hawes turned back around to Scotty, pointing again at his center mass.

"I'm sorry," Scotty said, aiming for his chest and pulling the trigger.

The lack of a good brace, owing to the missing finger, sent the bullet searing through Hawes's shoulder. It burned, like fire, and the force of the hit spun Hawes, like it had Tran, and he fell to his knees.

Behind him, he heard the gun hit the ground, then Scotty's body hit the side of the car, collapsing back against it with heaving sobs, Helena trying to quiet him.

Then Chris was in front of Hawes, helping him down onto his side, face pale with worry.

"I sold it." Hawes patted his breastbone, or rather the Kevlar over it, underneath his dark dress shirt. "But he was supposed to shoot me in the chest."

Chris heaved a half sob, half-relieved chuckle. "It wasn't your head, so I'll take it."

Speaking of his head, Hawes's felt woozy, light, like the

whiteout from the pain was spreading through the rest of his body.

Chris scooted behind him, holding his body up, a wad of fabric pressed to his shoulder. "Hang on, baby."

"Give the order to Kane," Hawes said to whoever was still listening. "Take Rose into custody, and tell him to add conspiracy to commit murder to the charges."

"On it, Big H," Holt said.

"Good," Hawes mumbled as pain and exhaustion grew heavy, too heavy to hold his eyes open against any longer. Once he heard Kane's, "You're under arrest," over the comm, he turned his face into Chris's neck, smelling eucalyptus and leather. "It's over."

"It's over," Chris said, his warm lips pressed against Hawes's temple, easing him into the darkness. "The empire is yours."

"Ours," Hawes said, then for the first time in three years, he rested.

CHAPTER FOURTEEN

Being on this side of the hospital bed sucked, maybe even worse than being the one in it, which Chris remembered all too well as it had been him there only three days ago. Hell, the surgeon who'd worked on Hawes's GSW was the same one who'd mended him. Once Hawes was in post-op, she'd insisted on checking Chris's injury and wouldn't let him into Hawes's room until she'd wrestled his arm back into a sling. But that had been hours ago, and while Chris's arm did feel better, his heart and head worried over the too still form in the bed.

He scooted closer and reached out his good hand, laying it on Hawes's hip, hoping this time, unlike the dozens of others, it would wake him. It didn't. Hawes's injuries weren't life-threatening. The GSW was a through and through, no major arteries hit, but as with Chris last week, Hawes's mind and body had suffered more than just physical injuries. He needed time to recover. And as long as he was here, Chris would be too.

His head had just hit the bed next to Hawes's hip when a soft knock sounded against the door. He was halfway out of the chair when Tran slipped inside and waved him back down. She didn't come any closer, though, leaning against the wall next to the door. A safe bet, as Chris's anger still simmered. It hadn't exploded yet—he was too tired for that—but it was there, bubbling beneath the surface.

"Rose is in custody," Tran said. "We picked up Brewster too."

The former Chris knew about, the latter was welcome news. "That's good."

When he didn't say anything more, she nodded toward Hawes. "How's he doing?"

"Doc says fine. He just hasn't woken up yet."

"Payback's a bitch."

If not for his anger, if not for the exhaustion, Chris probably would have laughed at her attempted joke—something he'd never thought he would hear from Vivienne Tran—but as pissed and tired as he was, the weak attempt at humor fell flat. He cut to the chase. "How's Scotty?"

"Sleeping, which is better than him being awake and in a world of hurt."

Chris was afraid of that. Wheeler had looked like hell on the scene, and it had only gone to shit from there. "How bad?"

"Broken ribs, punctured lung, head trauma. And there's risk of sepsis and gangrene from the GSW he was still recovering from."

"And his finger?" Chris asked, a phantom pain making his pinkie finger tingle in sympathy.

"Still missing."

Chris picked up Hawes's left hand, held it in his, thumb running over the knuckles of all five fingers. "At least it wasn't his dominant hand."

"He shouldn't have been injured at all." Sighing, she collapsed into the chair on the other side of the bed. "That's on me. I should have trusted you."

"Not me. Amelia. She's the one you should have trusted. She came through for us, multiple times."

"You're right." She drove a hand into her hair, grabbing a huge hunk of it and tugging. "Fuck, this could have been worse than Izzy's murder. That was the last thing I wanted."

Her voice vibrated with frustration, resignation, and anger, more than enough directed at herself. She didn't need Chris's piled on top of it—she knew she'd fucked up, she admitted it—and that was enough to cool Chris's bubbling fury. "You wanted justice for your wife," he said. "Things got tangled up. You didn't want to chance that."

Her dark eyes rose to meet his. "You didn't get tangled up."

"Oh yeah, I did," Chris said. "You just missed that part."

The corners of her mouth tipped up, but only for a moment, before her expression turned inward again. "How'd you find your way out of it?"

He closed his hand more firmly around Hawes's. "I

chose to trust him and that what I felt for him was real. The rest flowed from there."

Her gaze drifted to the window while her fingers toyed absently with the chain around her neck. Chris wondered if she realized she was doing it, if she realized she was this far from her usual locked-down self.

"You'll find it again too," he said. "Someday."

She let the chain go and gathered up her hair, all of it this time, and secured it in a bun at the base of her neck. Putting herself back together. "Your instincts were right, Perri," she said as she stood. "About Hawes, about Amelia, about this entire operation. Which is why I'll be recommending you to a field leader position. You earned it."

Chris didn't hesitate to tell her, "I'm out."

She froze mid-zip of her leather jacket. "You're out?"

"Of the agency," he clarified, even though her response indicated she'd understood him just fine. "Once we tie up all the back-end work on this case, I'll be resigning, officially."

Her gaze darted to Hawes, then back to him. "They're out of the explosives business. They're no longer the ATF's concern. It's not a conflict of interest, as far as I'm concerned."

"It is for me, with what I want for my life. I want to be here, in our city." He glanced out the window, then at Hawes. "With him, his family, my family, and maybe *our* family in the future."

"You're a damn fine agent, Perri."

He stood and met her at the end of the bed. "And I was

a damn fine private investigator too. Think I might give that a try again."

"You know..." The hint of a smile from earlier returned, growing wider this time. "Izzy once told me you were wasting your talents at the ATF, but she liked working with you too much to tell you that."

He chuckled. "Sounds like her."

Tran placed a hand on his forearm, and his laughter died. "She'd want you to be happy. I hope the PI gig—all of it—works out for you." She removed her hand, the personal connection fleeting, then vanishing completely as she held the same hand out to him, purely professional. "If you ever want to come back, I'll make it happen."

He shook her hand. "Thank you."

Help her, Izzy pleaded as Tran turned to leave.

"Vivienne," Chris said, startling her to a stop. "She'd want you to be happy too."

Tran rotated back to him, expression bleak as she tumbled the wedding rings in her palm. "Moving on from the love of your life is harder than the books and movies make it seem. I hope you never have to."

She left him with that painful thought, with the memory of the pinches of it he'd felt twice now—after the apartment explosion when he thought Hawes dead, and after Hawes had been shot today, even though he'd known the latter hadn't been fatal. He couldn't imagine what it would feel like to have Hawes ripped away for good, his heart torn out from his chest.

"I hope so too," came a scratchy voice from behind him.

Chris spun, finding Hawes awake, finally. Blue eyes tracked him all the way to the side of the bed. "Is this for real?" Hawes asked.

"Yeah, baby." Chris leaned down and dropped a kiss on Hawes's cool lips, so very relieved to feel them moving beneath his again. "This is for real."

Hawes had drifted in and out of consciousness most of the afternoon. Familiar voices and the drugs in his system had kept him in a comfortable state of mostly asleep, until Tran's relatively unfamiliar tone had caught and held, dragging him out of the fog. But he'd kept his eyes closed, pretending to sleep. He didn't want to interrupt. Chris and Tran's conversation had seemed important, for both of them, and for Hawes. He'd almost ruined the ruse and gasped aloud at Chris's verbal resignation. Granted, Chris had mentioned he was out when this was over, but telling it to friends and family was one thing, to his boss was another.

Staring at him now, Chris's dark eyes full of love, conviction, and relief, Hawes knew he meant it. No question. This was for real.

Chris gave him another too brief kiss, then handed him a glass of water. "How you feeling?"

Hawes sipped through the straw and swirled the cool water in his mouth, coating the parched surfaces. "Better than Scotty, sounds like."

"You were listening?"

Hawes took a longer swallow, then handed the glass back to Chris. "In and out."

"His recovery is going to be tough," Chris said, lowering himself into the chair next to the bed. "But he'll make it. How about you?"

Hawes tried to move his immobilized right arm and winced, pain like an arrow through his shoulder. Fuck, that hurt. "Believe it or not, this is the first time I've been shot."

"I believe it." Chris smiled, sly and heated. "No scars anywhere else I've seen, except the knife one here." He pushed up Hawes's sleeve, running his finger along the jagged, raised scar on his left shoulder. Goose bumps rose all over Hawes's skin.

"Helena," Hawes told him.

Chris chuckled, the sound warm and more comforting than the drugs. "That I also believe. But you still didn't answer my question."

"It's sore," he admitted. "And I won't believe you if you say yours isn't still." He fiddled with the matching strap across Chris's chest. "I think maybe we should both take some time off to recover."

"Agreed." The smile that had teased Chris's lips faded, the lighter mood too ephemeral to hold on to.

Hawes coasted his fingers farther up the strap of Chris's sling, close to the spot where Hawes had shot him three days ago. "I can't relive this again." He dropped his hand. "And we still need to talk about the first time I lived it, with Izzy. You need to know what happened, see it for yourself, before you upend your life more than you already have."

"The future means more to me than the past. It's not going to change—"

Hawes stilled Chris's shaking head with a hand on his cheek. "I hope it won't." Correction. "I'm trusting it won't." Chris calmed, though his eyes remained wary. "But as we go on from here, if you're the only one without the full story, that's not fair. That'll breed resentment, feelings of exclusion, and that's the last thing I want between us."

"You're talking about the video from the night Izzy died."

He had been, but that wasn't the only problem they had to tackle. "So it was a video on the other flash drive Amelia left?"

Chris nodded.

"We need to watch that too, then. I need to know how deep my grandmother's treachery ran. And Izzy deserves justice. So do we."

Chris averted his gaze as he picked up Hawes's hand and entwined their fingers. "We can wait—"

Hawes squeezed his fingers. "Now, please. I don't want this hanging over us any longer."

"All right." Chris stood, untangled their fingers, and fished a flash drive out of the coat hanging on the back of his chair. "Holt consolidated and made backups," he explained, plugging the chip end of the drive into his phone. "Screen's not ideal."

"It'll do." Hawes pushed himself up and over, making room on the bed for Chris to sit next to him. The warm body pressed alongside his was another comfort, one

Hawes desperately hoped would remain there after they watched these videos.

He had to trust... But it was hard once Chris clicked on the file labeled the day before Hawes's thirtieth birthday. Harder still as a picture appeared of that dark, rain-slicked street, as the phone speaker emitted the squeal of tires, the shouts between him and Zander Rowe, then the gunfire. The hardest when, after those few awful seconds of quiet, the truck door banged open and gunfire erupted again.

Chris's body jerked, and Hawes held his breath through his own recorded cries, the argument with Helena, and the fading roar of her Ducati. He hadn't even realized he'd closed his eyes and turned away until Chris's "Look at me" rumbled into the present silence. Like thunder, it was dark and ominous, and Hawes feared the accompanying lightning, what it might strike and destroy, how it might blind if he obeyed that order and looked at the man he loved. Did that man still love him? Hawes wanted to trust that promise so badly, but...

Rough fingers grasped his chin, no longer giving him an option. Hawes wasn't surprised by the tears on Chris's face or the anger in his eyes. But the words he spoke, "You didn't murder her," made Hawes inhale sharply.

"I pulled—"

"In self-defense."

"She was beaten and tortured, like Scotty." Hawes would never forget the marks around her wrists and the bruises on her face. He'd noticed them too late. Because he'd noticed the gun pointing at him instead. "She was just trying to escape."

"Maybe," Chris said. "But in order to do so, she had to kill you. Same as Scotty was set up to do today."

"Chris, what—"

The fingers gripping his chin eased, becoming a caress along Hawes's jaw, soothing him, soothing them both. "She was my partner, Hawes. We weren't in the field a lot together, but it was enough that I know what she looks like when she's frightened versus when she knows exactly what she's doing. She was more composed than Scotty was today."

Hawes's pulse raced, reflected in the rapid *beeps* of the heart monitor. "Are you saying this is the latter? Like Scotty?" He had never considered this scenario. The evidence to the contrary had seemed so cut-and-dried. But none of them knew Isabella like Chris did.

"I have no reason to lie. I'd already forgiven you, when you thought you'd murdered her. And I don't need to protect her either."

Hawes lifted a hand and brushed away the tears at the corners of Chris's eyes. The wetness was cool, but the eyes themselves were burning with fury. Despite Chris's gentle touches, that fire in his eyes had only mounted as they'd talked, as they'd analyzed with fresh eyes what they'd seen on that video. "Then why are you so angry?"

"Because my partner was going to kill you, then and today, because of something Rose held over them."

Hawes took Chris's hand in his, some instinct telling him to hold on tight. "You didn't know me then."

"If she had succeeded with Izzy, I wouldn't know you now. And Izzy would have never forgiven herself." Chris squeezed his hand so tight Hawes thought his fingers might break. "Rose would have taken you both away from me."

It was everything Chris could do not to bolt out of that hospital room and go straight to the station where Rose had been taken after her arrest. Only Hawes's hand wrapped in his and the investigator side of his brain kept him on that bed. Kept him wanting to know what was on that video dated the day before the one they'd just watched. It had to be the reason Izzy set out that night to kill Hawes. And Chris was sure that's what she'd meant to do. Her hold on the pistol, despite her injuries. The sharp angle of her clenched jaw. The desperation and determination in her eyes. In only a few seconds, Chris had recognized the danger, as had Hawes, who'd instinctively reacted to defend himself.

But why were they in that position at all? Rose had to have had something on Isabella, and as far as Chris could reason, it was one of two things: a case asset or himself. This had to be why she'd gone dark in the days before her death. Because Rose had taken her, worked her over, and forced her hand. Like she'd done Scotty. Fuck, if they had watched this before the op this morning could they have anticipated Rose's manipulation? Scotty's appearance on scene? Hawes had wanted to, but Chris had said no. He'd had his reasons, but if things had gone wrong this morning, if it had cost Hawes his life...

"Christopher." His full name, in Hawes's command

voice, snapped him out of his spiraling thoughts. Hawes shifted closer, his eyes anxious and full of concern. "You've got enough on Rose already. Maybe we just forget that other video exists."

Chris knew what he was trying to do. Protect him, protect them. But Chris was too far into this—three years of his life into it—to turn back now. "I want to know the whole truth. I have to."

"But what if it's something you can't come back from?" A shiver wracked his body, belying the control he'd injected into his voice.

Chris inhaled deeply, calming himself, and slung an arm around Hawes's shoulders. "I think I need you to do that for me this time. I need you to keep me steady."

A long stare-down ensued, but Chris wasn't giving in. Hawes eventually realized that and relented. Removing his arm from around Hawes, Chris retrieved the phone and held it between them once more. Hawes wound his good arm around Chris's waist, and Chris pressed Play.

An image filled the screen, and Hawes held him tighter.

Izzy was tied to a chair, arms wrenched behind her, feet secured to the posts. Her face was mottled with bruises, her nose was bleeding, and her shirt was dappled with spots of red.

"That's the warehouse," Hawes said. "One of the storerooms where we kept the explosives."

Amelia entered the picture behind Isabella. She dug into a pressure point on Izzy's back, and Izzy struggled in her restraints. Tears leaked from the corners of her scrunched-closed eyes, and her upper teeth chewed at her bottom lip. She didn't speak. Didn't make a sound.

"Enough," Rose said. Calm, like someone telling a waiter that was enough water.

Amelia backed off, and Izzy slumped in her chair. Head falling forward, she added tears and more blood to the canvas her shirt had become.

Rose stepped into the frame, immaculate in a designer suit, pearls on her neck and ears, not a hair out of place. "Let's try this again, Agent Constantine."

Izzy's eyes widened, too tired and tortured to hold back that tell.

Rose caught it. "We know you're not just a secretary. You're an ATF agent. A good one too. You almost succeeded where others have failed. You figured out to whom we were really going to sell those weapons. You even had an admirable plan to intercept them. But no one received it. We cut off your communications three days ago. No notes or contact. You've gone dark. Do you know what the feds think about agents who go dark?"

"I'm not dirty," Izzy seethed.

"I think they'll see it differently, especially with you in that truck with Zander tonight."

"I'm not—"

"You will." Rose stepped closer, daring Izzy to make a futile move from her position. "Or I will have your partner murdered."

Izzy lurched forward, and so did Chris. Amelia hauled Izzy back, a grip on her collarbone that made her scream. Hawes hauled Chris back, an arm around his chest and a kiss on his shoulder that made him whimper. Helplessly trapped in the now as he watched his best friend, his partner, being tortured in the past.

Izzy tried to disavow him, but Amelia rattled off all his pertinent details. Real name, badge number, address—real and undercover. "He's not here now," she said. "But he's got a niece that checks on his condo."

Fucking hell, Rose and Amelia had known all along. Who he was, where he lived, where his family lived. She still knew it.

On-screen, all the fight drained out of Izzy, her body folding in on itself as much as the bindings would allow. "Fine," she conceded. "Just leave Chris and his family alone, please."

"You do what I ask," Rose said, "and no harm will come to them."

"Why not just kill me?" Izzy asked. "Rowe can deliver—"

Rose shook her head, smile patient, like she was indulging a toddler. "This is the part of the plan you didn't know. Why I need you there too. Zander's not going to deliver those weapons tonight. He's going to die. By my grandson's hand."

"Hawes?"

"And once Hawes kills Zander, you're going to kill him."

Izzy paled, making the bruises and cuts on her face stand out in sharp relief. "Unless he kills me first."

"If he does, then he goes to prison for murdering a fed."

Except Holt and Kane had made sure that didn't

happen. They'd erased the incident footage, erased all evidence of Hawes's presence at the scene that night, and Rose's coup had been put on hold for three years.

Hawes took the phone from him as the video finished, the room going dark and Izzy's cries the only sound left. "She said she would handle us," Hawes said softly.

Chris's voice was not. "And now I'm going to handle her." The investigator side of him satisfied, neither Hawes's hand nor his body were enough to stop Chris any longer. Not when he was powered by pure fury.

"*Dante, no!*"

He ignored the twin shouts, from Hawes on the bed and Izzy in his head. Instead, it was something Scotty had said that rang loud in his mind.

Time to slay the fucking queen.

CHAPTER FIFTEEN

K ane was waiting for him around the corner from the holding rooms where Rose, according to the desk officer, had just met with her attorney. "Perri, you don't want to do this."

"Yeah, Brax, I do." Chris charged forward, intending to barrel right past him, and much like in his hallway yesterday, Chris found himself with his back to the wall and Kane immobilizing him with an arm across his chest. Chris struggled to wrench free and got nowhere. Even with both arms free, his sling discarded in the hospital parking lot, he was no match for the lean and wiry chief. Twenty plus years in the military, doing God only knew what, then a career in law enforcement, had taught Kane a maneuver or two.

"I'm trying to make sure you don't hurt yourself," Kane said. "Or those we care about."

"That's exactly why I'm here," Chris said. "She used me as leverage, against my own partner and best friend.

Then she did the same to Scotty. We can't let her do that again."

"Who's to say she will?" Kane countered. "She could have called in my badge or had me attacked at any time this past week, but she didn't."

"Because that was the condition of Hawes's deal with her. He'd do her bidding, and no harm would come to you."

Kane's hazel eyes grew wide. "Me? Why?"

The press of his arm slackened, the surprise distracting him, but not enough for Chris to fight free. Chris figured his answer, though, the truth none of them spoke but all of them knew, would do the trick. "Because if she hurt you, Holt would either fall apart or kill her himself. Hawes was protecting both of you."

Kane staggered backward like he'd been punched in the gut. Chris shot off the wall and hauled ass toward the holding rooms, throwing over his shoulder, "She's fucked with all of us for the last time."

Lost in the rising tide of anger, Chris rounded the corner and nearly ran into Holt, who wore a stunned expression. His massive form was impossible to get past, as were his questions.

"Is that true? What Hawes did? The deal—"

"Why would I lie about that? And was he wrong?"

Holt's gaze drifted past Chris, toward the corner. "He saved me."

Chris didn't think he was talking about Hawes. But Hawes's future was on the line here, as was Kane's. "And now I'm asking you to save both of them."

Holt's eyes snapped to his, gazes clashing for a long moment in which Chris wasn't sure what the big man would do, and then he stepped aside.

To Chris's right, a door swung open. Amelia stood over the threshold with Lily in her arms, and behind her, Oakland Ashe, Melissa Cruz, and the local US Attorney sat at the table.

Fucking hell, if Cruz and that ex-SEAL prosecutor got out here and got ahold of him, there'd be no escaping. Not wasting another second, Chris ran flat out to Rose's holding room, darted inside, and slammed the door shut behind him. He had just gotten a chair wedged under the knob when a *thump* hit the other side of the door, rattling it and the observation window in the adjacent wall.

"Agent Perri," a cool, calm voice said behind him.

Chris turned to face the devil herself. Or at least the devil that had been fucking with him for the past three years. What he hated most was that he fucking owed her at the same time. He would have never found Hawes had she not set all of this in motion. But in doing so, she might have taken him forever, along with Izzy. Might have taken Scotty too.

"Perri!" Kane shouted through the intercom, along with more banging on the door and on the observation window. Chris ignored it, flipped off the intercom, and claimed the chair across from Rose.

"I won't be Agent Perri for much longer."

"You did seem to wear Dante better." She smiled, like she had at Izzy in that video, and Chris wanted to wipe the smug look off her face. Mostly because she was right.

"I'll give you that," he said. "Your ability to read certain aspects of people. What makes them tick. Otherwise, you wouldn't have been able to move us around your board for so long. Wouldn't have been able to leverage me against Izzy."

"Ah, so that's why you're here," Rose said, folding her cuffed hands in her lap. The guard had neglected to secure them to the loop in the table. Intentional? Or just too stupid to realize this seventy-something woman was the most dangerous person in the building?

It made his next move even riskier. He made it anyway. Reaching inside his jacket, he removed his service weapon from its holster and set it on the table. Banging on the door and window intensified. Chris raised his voice to talk over it. "You manipulated all of us, over and over again,"—his gaze flickered to the gun—"because of that."

"My actions had nothing to do with a gun."

"But they did, didn't they? That was the final straw. That was the final weakness you couldn't abide. That your grandson chose to do his job as ethically as he could, without the symbols of power you knew. The guns, the explosives, contracts with clients who lived in the past with you. Outdated symbols, outdated methods and ideas that create too much collateral damage and cost innocent lives." Chris shook his head. "Moving beyond all that wasn't weakness—it was strength."

"Then why are you brandishing a gun now?"

He leaned forward, forearms on the table. "To end this."

The supposedly dead speaker crackled, and Hawes's strained voice filled the room. "Dante, don't, please."

Holt, Chris suspected, had overridden the electronic controls.

And given Rose a last playing card, or so she thought, judging by the Cheshire cat grin that stretched across her face. "He knows you wore it better too."

"Except it's not one or the other, Rose. It's both. It's me."

"Chris, please," Hawes begged. "Remember what you said. The future means more than the past."

"Hawes," Chris said, splitting his attention between his partner on the intercom and the threat across the table, "do you trust me?"

Hawes answered without hesitation. "Yes."

"Do you trust me to do the right thing here?"

"You're angry—"

"Do you trust me?"

"Yes." No more equivocation.

He shifted his attention fully back to Rose. "As well as you read people, that right there is what you never understood. Trust. Your grandchildren do. I do. Hell, even Amelia does. That's where our power, our strength, comes from. I don't need a gun for that. I don't ever want to touch one again." Hawes's sharp inhale echoed through the speaker, his own philosophy taken up by Chris as well. The banging had also ceased, a sign of their observers' shared trust. Confident, his team at his back, Chris smiled as he carried on. "All I need to be strong and powerful is your grandson, the rest of his family, and mine. People I love and trust to have my back. That's all any of us need. And if you ever come for us again, if you ever think to leverage one of us against the other, all that power will be directed against you. Do you understand?"

She shifted in her chair, a first sign of discomfort, but she lifted her chin, grasping at her last perceived straw of control. "He's lucky to have found you. Or rather, lucky I gave him to you."

"Bullshit," Hawes bit out. "You didn't do that. Isabella Constantine did."

And just like that, the last weight lifted off Chris's chest. Hawes was right. The connection he'd discovered with the man on the other end of the intercom wasn't owed to Rose. It was Izzy who had brought them together. Chris's anger vanished, snuffed out by love and appreciation for his old partner, who'd helped him find his new one. "Turns out Izzy saved my life, not once but twice. You don't get to steal that from her—from us. And you don't get to steal the Madigan legacy from your family. All you've stolen is your own chance to watch your grandchildren take that legacy, update it, and thrive. Maybe one day you'll understand that." He stood, reclaimed and holstered his weapon, then pushed in the chair. "And make no mistake, that's my legacy now too, and if you ever threaten us again, I will defend it at my partner's side."

Blue eyes met his, and they were just as cold as when Chris had walked in there. But the ice couldn't touch him, not with Hawes's "I love you" from the intercom warming every part of him and carrying him out the door and into his future.

CHAPTER SIXTEEN

Four Months Later

Chris was late, and his sister was gonna kill him. He'd been the instigator of this idea, and then when the date had finally arrived, he couldn't get here on time. Not that she didn't have half a dozen other hands helping her plan and prep, but still, he was gonna catch hell. Even if it wasn't his fault his flight was delayed. He pushed open the heavy glass door at Restaurant Gary Danko, and a chorus of *"Happy Birthday"* reached his ears.

"Mr. Perri," the hostess greeted with a warm smile as she took his coat. "I don't think I need to show you to your table this time."

Chris returned her smile. "I'm pretty sure it's all of them." They'd bought the place out for a double birthday party—Mia's and Lily's. Lily's first birthday landed two days before Mia's sweet sixteen, a reason to celebrate for both of them and their families. Granted, Lily, asleep in her father's arms, wouldn't remember any of this, but Mia, holding court at the center table in the half of the dining room they were using, seemed to be having the time of her life. She wore a "Sweet Sixteen" tiara and, with help from Gloria and Jax, was passing out cannoli and birthday cake to the Perris and Madigans gathered to celebrate.

"Perri," someone called from behind him.

Chris turned to find Scotty Wheeler emerging from the shadows of the empty half of the restaurant. It had been more than a month since Chris had last seen him, when they'd presented to the judge at Rose's sentencing. She had pleaded guilty to avoid a trial, but the federal prosecutor had not gone easy on her in sentencing. They'd laid out all the evidence Scotty and Jax had assembled against her, detailed Scotty's captivity, and each provided statements as to the events that had led to Rose's arrest.

Scotty had looked half-dead the entire time they'd been working, surviving pot of coffee to pot of coffee, and avoiding Chris at every opportunity. Gone was the newly found friend, replaced with a robot who just wanted to work in his own office with the door closed.

Now, "half-dead" was being generous. Scotty's hair was overlong and tousled, his eyes puffy, red-rimmed slits of brown, and his pale cheeks were rough with stubble. The thrown-together outfit was also uncharacteristic— jeans that fit too loosely, a wrinkled dress shirt, and an overcoat buttoned unevenly. He looked barely any better than when he'd checked out of the hospital, against medical advice.

"What did we say about calling me Chris?"

"Shit. I'm sorry, Chris." He fiddled with the wrinkled collar of the shirt, smoothing it down like he'd just realized it wasn't pressed. "And I'm sorry to crash."

"Scotty, you look..."

He gave up on the collar and scrubbed his hands over his face and into his hair. "Like I haven't slept for four months? Because that's about right." He dropped his hands, opened his mouth to say something else, but then from behind them, Hawes called, "Chris, is that you?"

Chris rotated sideways, enough that Hawes caught sight of the person he was talking to and his steps faltered. Chris suspected more from shock at how haggard Scotty looked than at his presence here or from some leftover animosity. Hawes carried none of that, but Scotty still suffered the guilt from it. "I'm sorry to crash," he repeated to Hawes. "I just wanted to apologize."

Hawes reached Chris's side, sliding an arm around his waist as he addressed Scotty. "You have nothing to apologize for. We've told you that."

"I shot you," he said to Hawes, then to Chris, "I wasn't a good partner."

"You were the best partner I had since Isabella."

"I was the only one you had since Agent Constantine."

"Because I wouldn't work with anyone else."

"And you shot me," Hawes said, "because you didn't have a choice."

"I keep replaying it..."

"Are you seeing someone? A therapist?" Chris asked. "The agency has resources."

Scotty nodded. "I've been going, weekly, but I'm leaving. The Bay Area. I'm taking some time off, now that my work on the case is done and the doctors have cleared me to travel."

"Scotty," Chris said gently, "your Southern is showing." He was tired and rambly, and the Southern drawl was coating his words, thicker than Chris ever remembered hearing it. It was attractive as hell, but he knew Scotty wouldn't think so. "Stop a minute and breathe."

That won a small smile. "Before I left, I needed to apolog—say thank you."

"Is there anything we can do to help?" Hawes said.

Scotty raked a hand through his hair, tousling it more. "I'm not sure anyone can help me right now."

The blunt admission of helplessness would have made Chris stagger if Hawes hadn't been holding him steady. As it was, it temporarily robbed him of a response. But not Hawes.

"Sam, maybe?"

Scotty's gaze, which had drifted toward the door, shot back to Hawes.

"Where are you really going, Scotty?" Hawes asked.

"There's more than one nightmare I need to sort out."

Recovering from his surprise, Chris stepped forward and tugged a startled Scotty into a hug. "When you do need us, call. We'll be there."

At his side, Hawes clasped Scotty's shoulder. "We're family, and we will always be there, for whatever you need."

Scotty sniffled a little. "Thank you both."

"Thank you," Hawes said. "For trusting me, and us."

Scotty smiled, stronger than the one before. "I'm glad he was right about you."

They shared another round of smiles, of hugs and handshakes, and then Scotty disappeared out the door. Chris's worry, however, didn't disappear with him. "Remind me to have Holt put a flag on him."

"Monday," Hawes said with a pat to his ass. "When you're officially back at work."

Chris turned into him, dipped his face, and gave Hawes the kiss he'd turned his lips up for. "Sorry I'm late. Flight was delayed." Chris stole another kiss, making up for the two weeks they'd been apart while he'd been at Glynco, then in DC, officially retiring from the ATF.

"You made it," Hawes said. "That's what matters."

"Celia feel that way?"

Hawes took him by the hand and led him toward the party. "She's too pissed at my sister to be pissed at you."

That was news, proven by the two women very obviously, and very intentionally, sitting on opposite sides of the room from each other. Which was the opposite of how they'd been acting the past few months. Chris had it on good authority that Helena was the shop's best new customer, "What's that about?"

"Helena's icing her out for some reason. And they're not the only ones." He jutted his chin toward the table where Chris had first spied Holt sitting with Lily. Kane was hovering nearby, but he wasn't sitting at the table with them, which in a group of family and friends was unusual.

"The visit with Amelia today at Dublin?" Amelia was still at FCI Dublin but serving a reduced sentence in minimum security in exchange for her cooperation on the investigation and for assisting Melissa Cruz on some open bounty matters.

Hawes shook his head. "No, that went fine. She got to spend time with Lily on her birthday and signed the separation papers. But those two"—his eyes flickered back to Holt and Kane—"have been off since everything went down."

Chris felt more than a twinge of guilt for contributing to the wall of tension between the two friends. It had been there since the day Chris had confronted Rose, when he'd told Kane and Holt about the deal Hawes had made to keep the chief safe. Chris wondered what would happen when the tension between them finally reached its breaking point.

"I never thought I'd be the most settled of the three of us," Hawes said, and Chris's guilt faded in light of the happiness he shared with Hawes.

"They'll sort it out." He nuzzled behind Hawes's ear, inhaling the scent he'd missed. "At least Lily is oblivious to it, and Mia is having a good time. That's all that matters tonight."

Chris couldn't agree more, and he didn't think he could be any happier either. His old family and his new one, together, and all of them healthy and for the most part happy. And he was back here with them, for good now. Home. He rested a hand at the small of Hawes's back, then slid it around to his hip. "Thank you for helping make this happen."

"Our family deserved to celebrate something good

after the past several months."

"*Our* family. Sounds good." He kissed Hawes's temple, unable to get enough of him. "I'd like to show you how thankful I am."

"Later." Hawes's blue eyes sparked with mischief. "I promise to give you something else to celebrate."

"It's Saturday," Chris bemoaned. "You're not supposed to be at work."

Hawes held the front door at MCS headquarters open for his partner. "How many Saturdays have I worked since we've been together?"

"All of them."

"Then what makes you think that's gonna change now?"

Chris grabbed him from behind as they waited for the elevator. "It's almost midnight." Kissed the groove of his neck. "I've been gone for two weeks." Nipped his ear. "Let's go home and fuck." Shoved his cock against Hawes's backside.

As tempting as all that sounded and felt, Hawes had something else he wanted to give Chris more. And he was fairly certain it would result in Chris's dick in his ass even faster than if they went home.

The elevator doors slid open, and Hawes tugged Chris inside. "This is my favorite time to be here," he told Chris as the elevator climbed to the third floor. Second shift on Saturdays was their last of the weekend. As the factory quieted, and as Saturday slipped into Sunday, it was like the whole world slowed down. When he was a kid, his parents or Papa Cal would use the time to catch up on paperwork, if they weren't on a job, and Hawes would tag along with them to MCS. While they worked, he would lie on the floor and stare out the windows, counting the stars in the sky when the fog allowed, or when it didn't, the stars in the water from the lights on the boats.

As an adult, he sat in the chair behind the desk and did the paperwork but still spent more time than he should staring out the windows. He enjoyed the time to unwind, to summon back the control the week had sapped away, to steady himself so he could do it all again. Except he had something even better than that now. The man pressed against his back, feeling him up and nuzzling behind his ear. "This that other celebration you mentioned?"

"Maybe..."

One of Chris's roving hands passed over where he'd been shot, and a shiver rolled through Hawes. Chris held him tighter, and before Hawes's mind could rewind too far, Chris's words pulled him back to the present. "Might have to fuck you first," Chris tempted, a hand lightly clasped around his neck and the other one not so lightly clasped over his cock. "Still haven't gotten the chance to fuck you in your office." He stroked Hawes's cock, and the friction through layers of silk about killed him. "Haven't been able to get that image out of my mind since the first time you brought me here. How I'd spread your arms and legs and bend you over, face first. Pin you down by the wrists and cover your body with mine. Ram my cock—"

Fuck, he was going to come too soon if he didn't shut the too tempting man up. He thrust back against Chris's dick, returning the torture, and tilted up his face for a kiss, demanding it.

Chris obliged, tongue down his throat, until the doors opened on the executive floor. "Been sittin' on that fantasy for months," Chris said as Hawes led them out of the cab.

Hawes stopped in front of the reception desk. "I want to make one adjustment."

"What's that?" Chris pushed him back against the polished wood. "On your back instead? Watch me as I fuck you?" He hitched up one of Hawes's legs. "Or do you want to ride me as I sit in your chair?" He grabbed Hawes's aching cock. "Or maybe you want to be the one fucking me?"

"Yes," Hawes gutted out, right at the edge again. "All of the above, but I want you to fuck me in *your* office."

Chris froze. "My office?"

Hawes slunk out from between the desk and Chris, took him by the hand again, and led him past Helena's and Holt's offices. He stopped in front of the new door in the line—four now where before there had been only three— and opened it for Chris.

Chris was silent as he walked into the new office, created from the more than extra space in Holt's and Hawes's offices. Hawes grew more nervous as the silence stretched on, to the point he felt compelled to fill it with words. "You've given me a place in your home." He'd moved into the condo in Mission Dolores last month. So

Hawes had made room for Chris at MCS too. "Now I'm giving you a place in mine."

Chris paused beside the desk and tapped the pink box on the corner. "Those what I think they are?"

"Mooncakes, yes, for celebration, I hope." He pointed at the mini fridge in the corner. "And there's champagne in there."

Chris continued on around the desk and inhaled sharply, his gaze landing on the framed pictures on the window ledge. Hawes crossed the room to stand beside him, to look again at the pictures of Ro, of Chris and his family, of Chris and Izzy at Glynco, and of them enjoying a couple beers after moving Hawes into the condo. "Gloria helped me with the pictures."

Chris lifted a hand and covered this mouth, whispering through his fingers, "Hawes, this is..."

Hawes looped an arm through his. "I didn't mean to presume, but you're out of the ATF now, working as a PI for us and for clients Mel refers. It makes sense for you to be here."

Chris shifted to face him, a brow raised. "Makes sense?"

"I want you with me, my partner at home and at work." He laid a hand on Chris's chest, over his heart that beat strong beneath his palm. "I never thought I'd have that, and a part of me is afraid it'll disappear one day, carried out by the fog."

"No, baby," Chris said, laying a hand over his. "The fog rolls in and out each day, but the Tower, the Pyramid, the Bridge, they're all still there before and after." He grasped

Hawes's hip with his other hand, squeezing in that place Hawes considered his. "And I will be too, every day."

"So that's a yes, to the office?"

"It's a yes to everything with you." Chris hauled him into a kiss that stole Hawes's breath, that wrapped him up so completely he startled when his ass hit the desk, Chris having picked him up and set him on the smooth surface. He shoved Hawes's legs apart and stepped between them, their bodies brushing, cock to cock, lips to lips. "And it's a yes to fucking you on my new desk before I cover it with work."

Hawes hitched his legs higher, drove his tongue deeper, and claimed the life that was his, that he never thought he would have. Then he gave himself to the man he wanted to share the rest of that life with. Lying back on the desk as he had in that warehouse four months ago, as he had against the ladder in his old condo during their first encounter. Arms spread, at Chris's tender, ruthless mercy, and feeling like the most powerful man in the world, like a king, as he let go and got lost, trusting that Chris would always be there—on him, in him, with him. By his side. A lover, a partner, the steadying force Hawes needed as he and his siblings rebuilt their new empire, this new legacy, one Hawes was proud to call their own.

For all the latest updates on new projects, sneak peeks, and more, sign up for Layla's Newsletter and join the Layla's Lushes Reader Group on Facebook.

A NOTE FROM LAYLA

Dear Reader,

Thank you for taking this *Fog City* journey with me. I hope you enjoyed Hawes and Chris's story as much as I did. And I hope you'll forgive me the cliffhangers as we made our way to this finale. I so wanted to do a project that was 100% me—an homage to the city I love and the action movies and episodic television I grew up on, including the dreaded to some, much beloved to me, To Be Continued. Thanks for your patience and support as I brought that dream to life in a series that I couldn't be more thrilled with.

So thrilled that I'm not quite ready to leave Fog City yet. While Hawes and Chris got their happily ever after, we've got some other folks to take care of still. Stay tuned for spin-offs! On that note, it wouldn't be a bad idea to check out my Whiskey Verse books in the *Agents Irish and Whiskey* and *Trouble Brewing* series, as you'll see more of those characters weave their way into the lives of our *Fog City* characters. The reading order and links for the complete Whiskey Verse are just a few pages over and also available at www.laylareyne.com.

Finally, reviews are an invaluable tool when it comes to spreading the word about great reads. Please consider leaving an honest review for *A New Empire* on Amazon, BookBub, or your favorite review site.

Thank you,

Layla

ACKNOWLEDGMENTS

Once again, Readers, especially my Lushes, thank you so much for your continued love and support for *Fog City* and for all my books. It's been a crazy year as I've ramped up the writing production, and your enthusiasm and encouragement kept me going.

Thanks again to the professionals who help make a gorgeous book, inside and out: Wander Aguiar and models, Patrick and Ryan, whose photo on the cover of this book, in particular, inspired the entire series; Cate Ashwood for taking that inspiration and creating such beautiful covers (including the award-winning cover of *Prince of Killers*); Kristi Yanta for the continued story guidance; Keren Reed for the prompt and careful copy editing; Susie Selva for always making my final drafts shine; and Leslie Copeland for assembling it all into this gorgeous package. Betas for this one get an extra round of applause, and their drink of choice on me, for the super short turn-around: Leslie, Erin, Allison, Kim, Rachel, Anna, and May. Thanks to Judith and the Novel Take team for always being a superb PR partner, and my continued appreciation to Tantor Audio and Tristan James for bringing *Fog City* to the all the audiophiles out there.

Finally, there are not enough *thank you*s in the world for the amazing author friends who have helped me through the ups and downs of self-publishing this past year. It's been a wild ride, but I'm sort of getting the hang of it, thanks to your wisdom and time so graciously given.

ALSO BY LAYLA REYNE

Dine With Me

Fog City:
Prince of Killers
King Slayer

Agents Irish and Whiskey:
Single Malt
Cask Strength
Barrel Proof
Tequila Sunrise
Blended Whiskey

Trouble Brewing:
Imperial Stout
Craft Brew
Noble Hops

Changing Lanes:
Relay
Medley

ABOUT THE AUTHOR

RITA Finalist Layla Reyne is the author of the *Fog City*, *Whiskey Verse*, and *Changing Lanes* series. A Carolina Tar Heel who now calls the San Francisco Bay Area home, Layla enjoys weaving her bi-coastal experiences into her stories, along with adrenaline-fueled suspense and heart-pounding romance. She is a member of Romance Writers of America and its Kiss of Death and Rainbow Romance Writers chapters. Layla is a RWA® RITA® Finalist in Contemporary Romance (Mid-Length) and Golden Heart® Finalist in Romantic Suspense.

You can find Layla at laylareyne.com, on Facebook, Instagram, and Twitter as @laylareyne, and in her reader group on Facebook—Layla's Lushes.

facebook.com/laylareyne

twitter.com/laylareyne

instagram.com/laylareyne

amazon.com/author/laylareyne

bookbub.com/authors/layla-reyne

CPSIA information can be obtained
at www.ICGtesting.com
Printed in the USA
LVHW082135230123
737806LV00031B/844

9 781734 175318